LOVE AND APOLLO

The great statue of Apollo which had fallen to the ground was gradually broken up and pieces were carried away to England and France.

Yet much of the statue, Valona knew, remained in Delos, but it lay too far for her to go and see.

Yet she was aware that it was still there and, as she had read, filled with a tremendous power.

One visitor to the statue had written,

"It was splendid in its loneliness, its perfect beauty and its terrible power."

Valona was a long way from it and yet as she stood looking towards the East, she felt the magic of the young God once thirty feet high.

She was sure she could see him with his parted lips, his uplifted hands and his eyes gazing out to sea.

More than two thousand years had passed by since Apollo's statue had been erected on the island and yet she knew just as if he was telling her, that time had in no way weakened him.

It was then that she began praying to Apollo with all her heart and soul.

She asked him that if one day he would give her the true love which she longed for and which he as the God of Light and Love represented to all who worshipped him.

'Help me, please help me!' she begged. 'The love I seek is the same love you give to the world and it is even more powerful than anything else mankind could possess.'

THE BARBARA CARTLAND PINK COLLECTION

Titles in this series

LOVE AND APOLLO

BARBARA CARTLAND

Barbaracartland.com Ltd

THE BARBARA CARTLAND PINK COLLECTION

Barbara Cartland was the most prolific bestselling author in the history of the world. She was frequently in the Guinness Book of Records for writing more books in a year than any other living author. In fact her most amazing literary feat was when her publishers asked for more Barbara Cartland romances, she doubled her output from 10 books a year to over 20 books a year, when she was 77.

She went on writing continuously at this rate for 20 years and wrote her last book at the age of 97, thus completing 400 books between the ages of 77 and 97.

Her publishers finally could not keep up with this phenomenal output, so at her death she left 160 unpublished manuscripts, something again that no other author has ever achieved.

Now the exciting news is that these 160 original unpublished Barbara Cartland books are already being published and by Barbaracartland.com exclusively on the internet, as the international web is the best possible way of reaching so many Barbara Cartland readers around the world.

The 160 books are published monthly and will be numbered in sequence.

The series is called the Pink Collection as a tribute to Barbara Cartland whose favourite colour was pink and it became very much her trademark over the years.

The Barbara Cartland Pink Collection is published only on the internet. Log on to www.barbaracartland.com to find out how you can purchase the books monthly as they are published, and take out a subscription that will ensure that all subsequent editions are delivered to you by mail order to your home.

NEW

Barbaracartland.com is proud to announce the publication of ten new Audio Books for the first time as CDs. They are favourite Barbara Cartland stories read by well-known actors and actresses and each story extends to 4 or 5 CDs. The Audio Books are as follows:

The Patient Bridegroom	The Passion and the Flower
A Challenge of Hearts	Little White Doves of Love
A Train to Love	The Prince and the Pekinese
The Unbroken Dream	A King in Love
The Cruel Count	A Sign of Love

More Audio Books will be published in the future and the above titles can be purchased by logging on to the website www.barbaracartland.com or please write to the address below.

If you do not have access to a computer, you can write for information about the Barbara Cartland Pink Collection and the Barbara Cartland Audio Books to the following address:

Barbara Cartland.com Ltd., Camfield Place,
Hatfield, Hertfordshire AL9 6JE, United Kingdom.
Telephone: +44 (0)1707 642629
Fax: +44 (0)1707 663041

THE LATE DAME BARBARA CARTLAND

Barbara Cartland who sadly died in May 2000 at the age of nearly 99 was the world's most famous romantic novelist who wrote 723 books in her lifetime with worldwide sales of over 1 billion copies and her books were translated into 36 different languages.

As well as romantic novels, she wrote historical biographies, 6 autobiographies, theatrical plays, books of advice on life, love, vitamins and cookery. She also found time to be a political speaker and television and radio personality.

She wrote her first book at the age of 21 and this was called *Jigsaw*. It became an immediate bestseller and sold 100,000 copies in hardback and was translated into 6 different languages. She wrote continuously throughout her life, writing bestsellers for an astonishing 76 years. Her books have always been immensely popular in the United States, where in 1976 her current books were at numbers 1 & 2 in the B. Dalton bestsellers list, a feat never achieved before or since by any author.

Barbara Cartland became a legend in her own lifetime and will be best remembered for her wonderful romantic novels, so loved by her millions of readers throughout the world.

Her books will always be treasured for their moral message, her pure and innocent heroines, her good looking and dashing heroes and above all her belief that the power of love is more important than anything else in everyone's life.

"If love comes from God, as I fervently believe it does, then it should not matter which God you are talking about. God is love and love is the nearest we will ever get to God, so I always advise my friends who are looking for love – every day close your eyes, pray as hard as you can to God and you will be rewarded by finding the love you seek."

Barbara Cartland

CHAPTER ONE
1887

The Duke of Inchcombe walked straight into his sister's boudoir to find her sitting at the writing table by the window.

She looked up and exclaimed,

"Oh, I see you are now back, Arthur. What was the funeral like?"

"Gloomy, as you might imagine," he replied, "and there were not as many people as I had expected."

Lady Rose got up from the writing table and moved across the room to the sofa.

"What am I going to do, Arthur," she asked, "about a Lady-in-Waiting?"

"I have been thinking about that while coming back to London. She will have to be someone discreet."

Lady Rose nodded her head and then she looked at him, a pleading expression on her face.

"*Must* I really do this? The whole idea horrifies me and you know how much I want to stay in England."

"I know, Rose, but if you do stay, you cannot go on as you are. People are sure to find out about it sooner or later."

"And what if they do?" she demanded defiantly.

"Then you will most certainly lose your reputation and if the older members of the family are told all about it, you can imagine what they will say."

Lady Rose made a helpless gesture with her hands and walked to the window.

Her brother sat down in a chair and looked at her.

She was very attractive with her hair glinting in the sunshine and her exquisite features silhouetted against the windowpane.

He was sorry, desperately sorry, at what she was being forced to do, but he could not think of any plausible alternative.

Lady Rose was nearly twenty years old and when she had 'come out' as a *debutante*, she had been an instant success.

And at the end of last year she had fallen in love.

Wildly, head-over-heels in love with the Marquis of Dorsham.

As he was only twenty-seven, extremely handsome and exceedingly rich, it would, the Duke knew, have been a perfect marriage in every way.

Unfortunately the Marquis at the age of twenty-two had been pressured into marriage.

At the time it had seemed such an excellent union and likely to prove happy.

The young girl the Marquis had married was one of the greatest beauties of the Season. Her parents were both in-waiting to Queen Victoria and they had been delighted at the marriage.

They had, however, omitted to tell the bridegroom that their daughter was at times given to strange seizures, which in some way had affected her brain.

It was not until after they had been married for two months that the Marquis discovered his wife's problem.

Later when he eventually realised the seriousness of the condition, the doctors were called in.

But it was too late – there was nothing they could do for the Marchioness.

Her seizures became more and more severe, until she was now permanently in the hands of her doctors and nurses. She did not even recognise her husband when he came to see her.

When he fell in love with Lady Rose, the Marquis realised exactly what he was missing.

They then both despairingly faced a future in which it was impossible for them to be together.

It was only by a miracle, the Duke reflected, that their love for each other had not been uncovered already.

There were those in Society who were always ready to find fault with anyone who was popular and if they had found out, the gossips would have all run straight to Queen Victoria.

Then, as the Duke had expressed it to his sister, 'the balloon would have gone up'.

As it was, the Queen had sent for Lady Rose with a very different proposition.

The political situation in the Balkans had been very unstable for some years.

It had now become even worse since the accession of Czar Alexander III to the throne of Russia.

He burned with indignation that Russia had not yet fulfilled her mission to dominate the Balkans and to seize control of the Dardanelles, which would give the Russians access to the Mediterranean.

Stubbornly and surreptitiously he pursued the same goals as the previous Czar and he was clearly determined to establish Russian-dominated Governments in Serbia and Greece.

The reports flowing into the British Foreign Office were particularly worrying.

The Russians secretly acted as *agents provocateurs* stirring up endless trouble in the established regimes of the Balkans and undercover agents would pose as icon-sellers, as Russian Embassy officials paid crowds to stir up riots.

Every report being sent back to England was worse than the last.

The climax of continuing horror was reached when Prince Alexander of Battenburg, the Ruler of Bulgaria, was abducted and forced at gunpoint to abdicate his throne.

There was only one country that Russia was afraid of and that was Great Britain and the Czar could not afford a war against Queen Victoria.

As soon as this was realised by the Queen and her advisers, she arranged marriages for the Kings and Princes of many Royal Principalities in the Balkans.

Several of her relatives were by now already sitting on foreign thrones and once the Union Jack was seen to be flying over a small country, the Russians quietened down or withdrew.

Her Majesty the Queen, however, was by now to all intents and purposes running short of supplies, because her remaining few relatives were either too young or already married.

When King Phidias of Larissa sent an Ambassador with a most urgent appeal to Her Majesty for help, she had thought she would have to refuse his request.

It was the Earl of Rosebery, Secretary of State for Foreign Affairs, who suggested Lady Rose Combe.

The Queen had quite forgotten that the late Duke of Inchcombe was married to one of her distant cousins, who had now been dead for over fifteen years.

The present Duke was surprised when the Queen sent for him for a private audience.

He was firmly told by Her Majesty that she wished to send his sister, Lady Rose, to Larissa.

"I will inform her, ma'am, what you suggest," said the Duke. "At the same time I feel sure she will not wish to leave England."

"Lady Rose must put her country first," the Queen instructed. "And as she has Royal blood in her veins, she will be aware of where her duty lies!"

The Duke considered that it would be a mistake to argue further with the Queen.

On his return home he was not surprised when his sister was horrified at the proposal and at first she insisted that she had no intention of obeying the Queen.

"Why," she demanded hotly, "should I be sent to marry some obscure Balkan King who no one has ever heard of?"

"I made a few enquiries," replied the Duke. "He is in fact quite an important King, although unfortunately not very young."

"What do you mean, *not very young*?" Lady Rose exploded.

"He is over fifty."

"And they expect *me* at *my* age to marry a man of *that* age?"

"Larissa is an important country, although I did not realise that until just now, Rose. It has vital access to the Mediterranean, which is, of course, what the Russians want and they are striving by every possible means to acquire."

"Well they will not acquire it through me," retorted Lady Rose stubbornly.

There was a pained silence, yet the Duke persisted,

"Now listen for a moment, Rose. I know you are in love with Gerald and he with you, but there is not a chance in hell of your ever being able to be married."

Lady Rose walked to the window and he knew that she was fighting against tears.

"It is *so* cruel," she moaned, "wicked and cruel that Gerald should be so tied up to this woman and there is no escape."

"I know that," the Duke sympathised.

"From what I have been told," his sister continued, "she might live for ever. After all she is still quite young and there is nothing wrong with her body. Only her mind is drastically affected."

"I know, I know, it is terribly hard and everyone who knows Gerald is very sorry for him. But what can we do?"

The Duke recognised without having to say it that a divorce was impossible.

The Marquis could not divorce his wife unless she was unfaithful to him and even then it would need a special Bill to go through Parliament.

And that would inevitably take a long time and also would cause a great deal of talk and scandal while the case was being heard.

But there was no provision in the divorce laws for a man to be rid of his wife because she was mad or unable in any way to perform the duties of a wife.

Even if he raised the matter in the House of Lords, it was impossible that any good would come of it.

However cruel it might be, the Marquis was in fact married for life to a young woman who did not even know who he was, but who bore his name.

"If you stay here," the Duke told her quietly, "and go on seeing Gerald as you do now, sooner or later people will notice it. Servants talk and, although Gerald is known to be my friend, women who are jealous of your beauty will soon begin to think it strange he is with us so much."

"But I must see him, *I must*," Lady Rose insisted.

"That is the whole point, Rose, it is torture to you to know he is in London when we are in London, and in the country when we are in the country and not be able to see him."

Lady Rose did not speak and after a moment the Duke went on,

"I honestly think, although you will not believe me at the moment, that it will be better for you to go away altogether."

"I would rather *die* than marry any other man," she screamed violently.

"As you cannot marry Gerald, does it really matter who you marry? If it had to be an arranged marriage, it might as well be to a King as anyone else!"

Lady Rose walked backwards and forwards across the room before she could reply to him.

She knew in her heart that she was fighting a battle she could never win.

It was really completely impossible, although they did not admit it in words, for either of them to refuse what the Queen was asking.

It was in effect a Royal command.

Finally Lady Rose sank herself down on the sofa and moaned helplessly,

"Very well, I will accept Her Majesty's suggestion on the one condition that Gerald is appointed to escort me to Larissa."

The Duke stared at her in astonishment.

"Do you think that wise, Rose?"

"I don't care if it is wise or not," she answered. "I want to be alone with Gerald before I finally leave him for ever. As you will know, someone of importance from the

Palace will be sent to escort me and represent the Queen. It is something Gerald has done several times in the past when other members of the Royal Family were pushed off to save the Balkans."

The Duke knew that this was true.

"I will try to arrange it and as Her Majesty knows we are great friends, she might accept the idea and say that I have to go too."

"But of course you must come with me, Arthur. I am not going to be left with any tiresome old courtier who will be very suspicious of Gerald and me from the moment he steps on board."

"Very well," he muttered, "I will try to arrange it."

He put out his hand and touched his sister's.

"I am so sorry, old girl, that this has happened. I would give everything I possess if I could help you."

"I suppose we shall somehow survive without each other, but it's not going to be easy."

"I think you are being very brave, my dearest Rose, and I am very proud of you."

Then in a different tone altogether, he added,

"Now that Sarah has died so unexpectedly, we shall have to find someone else to be your Lady-in-Waiting."

Lady Rose realised that he was right.

The Duke had suggested to the Queen that his sister would like to take her aunt, Lady Sarah Warren, who was a widow, to accompany her to Larissa.

The Queen had agreed, so there was no difficulty about the idea, but sadly Lady Sarah had died unexpectedly from a heart attack.

"Who can I have?" she asked. "It cannot be any of my own friends if Gerald is with us."

"No of course not – that would be disastrous."

The Duke suddenly gave an exclamation.

"Who have you thought of, Arthur?"

"I have just remembered that at yesterday's funeral, there was another relation – Princess Louise of Piracus."

Lady Rose thought for a minute.

"Yes, I believe she was a very distant cousin of our Mama. I do recall her staying with us once in the country about six years ago."

"She is now living in a Grace and Favour house at Hampton Court and she has her daughter with her who is, I gather, just eighteen."

Lady Rose did not speak, so he continued,

"I feel that as they are extremely hard up, I ought to do something about them. The next time I have a party in the country I will ask them both of them to stay."

"That will be very nice for them," she pouted, "but *I* shall not be there."

"I know, but I thought Valona, which is the girl's name, might be a good choice as your Lady-in-Waiting."

Lady Rose stared at him.

"It's not a bad idea. If she is living in a Grace and Favour house at Hampton Court, she is not likely to have heard any rumours about me and Gerald."

"She is also very young and I should think has no knowledge at all of the Social world. Certainly of nothing that might happen at Windsor."

"I have always been told that Her Majesty is rather mean to her Royal relatives for whom she has no particular use. But I am a bit surprised that she has not yet found a husband for Valona."

The Duke laughed.

"I think if the truth were known, Her Majesty has forgotten about them. I have never heard them mentioned when I have been at Windsor. Princess Louise is in fact a distant relative also of the Queen and a quite unobtrusive woman who would not have made any claims on her."

"Well, as we shall be doing her a kindness as well as making use of the girl, you had better suggest that she takes Sarah's place," proposed Lady Rose.

"It seems a great deal more satisfactory than having anyone who would be suspicious the moment she saw you and Gerald together."

"What do you mean? We are very discreet," Lady Rose riposted sharply.

"You may be able to control what you say, Rose, but you cannot control your eyes too. Anyone who is at all observant, and perhaps a little suspicious, would know by the way you look at each other that you are both in love."

"A lot of good it is doing us," she grated bitterly. "Oh, Arthur, how *can* I leave him? How could I possibly marry another? And how do you think I can live in a far off country where I will never even see him?"

There was a note in her voice that made her sound very pitiful.

The Duke put his arm round his sister protectively.

"I know just what you are feeling, Rose, it is not a question of how you can live elsewhere without him, but how you can just remain here without causing an appalling scandal that would hurt him abominably and undoubtedly would upset the whole of our family."

Lady Rose was silent for a moment before saying,

"You are right, of course, you are right, Arthur. I shall have to go and, if things are worse than I think they will be, I can always drown myself in the Mediterranean!"

"You are not to talk like that," he told her sharply. "Perhaps by some amazing miracle something will happen that will make things better than they are at this moment."

He was thinking that perhaps his sister would fall in love with someone else as he was certain that when she and the Marquis were apart for long enough, the agony would not be so intense.

They might even forget each other.

"When do I have to leave for this horrible hell of a place where I shall be utterly and completely miserable?" squawked Lady Rose.

"In ten days time and if you agree, I shall go and call on Princess Louise tomorrow and suggest that Valona accompanies you to Larissa.

"The girl's father was a Greek, so she will be able to speak that language. I believe that, like all the Balkan countries, Larissa contains a great deal of Greek in its own language."

"You had better arrange that there is someone to come with us," added Lady Rose, "who can at least tell me how to say 'good morning' or 'good night.' That is going to be difficult enough as I have never been good at foreign languages."

"Valona will be able to help you a great deal, Rose, and I really think we have made an excellent choice where she is concerned."

As he left his sister he was only hoping there would be no difficulties and that Princess Louise would allow her daughter to travel to Larissa.

He could see no reason why she should object and it could not be very much fun for a young girl to be living at Hampton Court in one of the Queen's Grace and Favour houses.

They were occupied by ancient diplomats or minor Royalty exiled from their own countries, who relied on the Queen of England to save them from starving to death.

The Duke drove to Windsor Castle the next day and asked for an audience with the Queen.

He told her that Lady Rose was deeply grateful to Her Majesty for her kindness, and she would consider it a great privilege to marry His Majesty King Phidias.

"I understand, ma'am," the Duke continued, "from Lord Rosebery that Your Majesty is generous enough to send us in a battleship to Larissa."

"I think that is important," the Queen replied. "It will make the Russians, who I understand are infiltrating into Larissa, aware we mean business if they try to force the King to abdicate and take over the country."

"I doubt after the way they behaved in Bulgaria to Prince Alexander of Battenburg, that they would go so far now as they did then. At the same time, just by infiltrating amongst the people they can foment riots and strikes. In fact they can make it impossible for the King to rule."

The Queen nodded.

"I am very aware of the situation in the Balkans and that is why I want your sister's marriage to take place as quickly as possible."

"We have been delayed, ma'am, by the sad death of Lady Sarah Warren, who was to become my sister's Lady-in-Waiting. I thought it would be a splendid idea, if Your Majesty will approve, to appoint the daughter of Princess Louise of Piracus, who is willing to take her place."

The Duke saw the surprise in the Queen's eyes and there was a pause before she replied, as she had obviously forgotten all about the very existence of Princess Louise.

The Queen possessed a very quick brain and where

her orders were concerned, she made as few difficulties as possible.

"I congratulate you, Your Grace, I did not think that Princess Louise's daughter was old enough for such a task. But if, as you say, she is ready to travel to Larissa, I am delighted to give my approval for her to be your sister's Lady-in-Waiting."

"Your Majesty is most gracious and my sister and I would be most grateful if Your Majesty would consider the appointment of the Marquis of Dorsham to represent Your Majesty at the wedding."

"The Marquis of Dorsham?" the Queen queried at once with a faint note of surprise in her voice.

Then she remembered that he was a close friend of the Duke.

"I see no reason, Your Grace, why he could not go. I believe he was very capable when he looked after one of my grand-daughters a year ago."

"I am sure he will be the same in Larissa, ma'am. "Once again I must thank Your Majesty on behalf of my sister and my whole family."

He bowed and kissed the Queen's hand and backed his way slowly from the room.

Once outside he thought with some satisfaction that he had carried off what could have been a rather difficult situation.

Rose had won her own way.

But it was more than that which pleased him as he left Windsor Castle.

It was obvious that the Queen had no idea of what his sister and the Marquis felt for each other.

She could not have heard even a whisper that they were interested in each other, let alone in love.

If she had heard anything she would undoubtedly never have agreed to the Marquis travelling with them to represent her at Larissa.

Her Majesty would have then produced an elderly, tiresome and garrulous courtier.

And Rose would have been even more upset than she was already.

'We are lucky in that if in nothing else,' the Duke ruminated as he drove down to Hampton Court.

He had believed it a mistake to ask Princess Louise first if her daughter could go to Larissa as he did not want to raise their hopes just in case the Queen had refused point blank to appoint anyone so young.

Now the Duke thought of it, Her Majesty had not asked Valona's age.

Had it been because she had forgotten all about the existence of her mother?

'That is yet another point on which we were very lucky,' the Duke mused to himself with a smile.

He knocked gently at the door and entered the small Grace and Favour house where Princess Louise lived.

He realised at first glance that she was very poor.

Her husband, His Royal Highness Prince Hermes of Piracas had been thrown off his throne by a revolutionary coup and had only escaped to England by the skin of his teeth.

He had, however, been badly wounded in the leg in the fighting which had taken place in his Palace and had died soon after his arrival in England.

The Royal couple and their child had come away in a wild hurry with no money and had thrown themselves at the mercy of the Queen.

She had given them a Grace and Favour house and a very small pension.

Then, as the Duke had found out, had forgotten all about them, but he could hardly accuse the Queen of being slightly inhuman to them.

He and his family had behaved no better.

Princess Louise had been busy nursing her husband when they had arrived in England, and the Duke's father, with whom she was distantly connected as well as with the Queen had shown very little interest in her.

In fact they had neglected her as well.

The Duke looked round the poorly furnished room and he thought that in making Valona a Lady-in-Waiting to his sister, he would be doing them a good turn.

It might make up in a small way for all the years of neglect.

The Princess came into the room and was surprised to see him.

"How very kind of you to call on me," she greeted him. "It was delightful to see you at the funeral, and I did hope for Valona's sake that we might have the chance of meeting you again."

"It is Valona I have come to see you about."

The Duke came straight to the point and Princess Louise invited him to sit down.

When he was seated he told her that his sister Rose was shortly going to Larissa to marry King Phidias and that Sarah, whose funeral they had both attended yesterday, had been intending to travel with his sister as Lady-in-Waiting.

Princess Louise was listening to him intently as he continued,

"As Valona is only a year or two younger than my sister, I thought that it would be very nice for them to be together. Her Majesty has given her permission for me to invite Valona to be Rose's Lady-in-Waiting."

Princess Louise looked astonished.

"It has never entered my mind that such a thing was possible!" she exclaimed.

"We will all be travelling in a battleship," the Duke told her, "and I promise you we will look after Valona very carefully and if after some months in Larissa she wishes to return, I will make every effort to find someone else to take her place.

"Naturally you will understand that it would be far more satisfactory for Rose and myself to have a relative in such a position of trust rather than a stranger."

"I understand," replied Princess Louise in her soft voice. "And I am so very grateful to you for having even thought of Valona. Shall I call her down and see what she thinks about your proposition?"

"Please do."

He stood up as the Princess rose and when she had left the room, he looked around.

He was thinking that as a family they had been very remiss in not taking more trouble over Princess Louise.

The room was most sparsely furnished and in fact its only real ornamentation was the number of books in it – not only on shelves but on tables and some were even piled on the floor as if there was no other place for them.

The Duke wondered if it was the Princess who was such an avid reader or her daughter.

The door now opened and the Princess entered with Valona beside her.

He had only had a quick glance at her yesterday at the funeral, but now he realised she was very pretty and if she was better dressed, she would undoubtedly be hailed as a beauty.

Valona was fair whilst her mother was dark and her eyes seemed to portray a touch of her Greek blood, which made them large and there was something definitely mystic about them.

The Duke felt that could be expected in a Goddess who came from Olympus.

Valona walked quickly over to him with her hand outstretched.

He realised that she was not the least shy.

"How lovely it is to see you again," she exclaimed. "When I saw you at the funeral I was thinking how proud we should be, Mama and I, to have such distinguished relatives."

The Duke laughed.

"And I was thinking the same about *you*!"

"I don't believe it for a moment, but I like to hear you say it."

They both sat down and the Duke explained exactly what he wanted Valona to do.

She was completely incredulous at the idea.

He knew it had never crossed her mind that he or his family could ever be interested in her.

"I would just love to be a Lady-in-Waiting to your sister, but perhaps I will not be very efficient."

"You will find plenty of people to tell you what to do when you reach Larissa, but you will undoubtedly find, Valona, just as I have, that protocol and all that bowing and scraping becomes very monotonous after a while."

"To me it will be something so new and thrilling," enthused Valona. "And, of course, I would love to go on a battleship. I adore being at sea."

"You are not seasick?"

"I do hope not. Mama said I was not sick when we came to England, but I was only ten at the time."

"Now you have to tell us," Princess Louise came in,

"is what clothes Valona will require. To be very frank, we have very little money."

"As Valona is one of the family," replied the Duke, "and I am the head of it, I think that I should be responsible for her. She must represent England in a way which will delight all the people of Larissa and make them even more impressed than they are at the moment by the Union Jack."

Princess Louise drew in her breath.

He could tell how worried she had been, wondering how Valona could possibly appear in public in the clothes she owned at the moment.

"I want you to be very sensible about it," the Duke went on, "and to spend however much is necessary to make Valona look smart and as beautiful as I know she will be if she has the right frame for her loveliness."

Valona clasped her hands together and exclaimed,

"That is the nicest and most exciting thing that has ever been said to me! Oh, thank you, thank you, Cousin Arthur, as Mama wishes me to call you. I think you are the kindest man who ever existed!"

"The only snag to all this is that you will have to work very quickly. My sister is leaving in nine days time."

Princess Louise gave a cry of horror.

"How can we do it?"

"Quite easily," he responded, "if you go to the best shops in Bond Street, I will give you their names."

He thought it very unlikely that the Princess had the slightest idea which they were.

He therefore wrote down the names of the shops his sister patronised and also a very attractive actress in whom he was interested supported the same shops.

He had bought her several gowns and had felt the money was well spent as she looked so lovely in them.

He gave the names to the Princess as well as a note saying the bills were to be sent to him.

"Show this note to the shops and you will have no difficulties. And you must not be offended if I give you some money now to hire a carriage to take you from here into London."

Thinking that the Princess was about to protest, he added quickly,

"If you are too proud to accept money, I shall have to send one of my own carriages and my coachman to take you out shopping. That, quite frankly, would be slightly inconvenient as my sister is using it at the moment to finish buying her trousseau."

Tears were sparkling in Princess Louise's eyes as she thanked him.

Then as he rose to depart, she remarked,

"I am just a little bit worried about your sister as I remember being told by one of the old Ambassadors living here who knows Larissa well that King Phidias has been ill for some time."

"We are only hoping that he will be well enough to enjoy his wedding, but as you must be aware, the Russians will be waiting for him to die and will then try to take over the country before he is replaced on the throne."

The Princess nodded.

"I was afraid that would be the situation."

"And that is why it means we must waste no time and be prepared to leave in nine days time."

"I will be ready, I promise you that I will be ready," exclaimed Valona. "And thank you so very much, Cousin Arthur, for being so kind. It will be so fantastic for me to have some really wonderful clothes. Mama finds it very hard to make all the dresses I need."

"I think that your mother has been very brave," the Duke told her. "And as soon as you have left for Larissa, I am going to suggest she comes to stay for a little while at Combe Hall in Norfolk. There are a number of my relatives there who will want to welcome her back into the family."

"It will be a great pleasure to meet them," said the Princess gratefully.

Her voice was a little unsteady and the Duke knew she was near to tears.

He expressed his goodbyes and kissed Valona.

"You are going to be my prettiest relative, Valona, and I am determined that all the family will admire you. They may have to wait until you come back from Larissa, but in the meantime you will be upholding the Union Jack and we shall be very proud of you."

Valona gave a little laugh and he noticed that she had dimples in both of her cheeks.

"I only hope that I shall understand such delightful compliments even if they are said in another language. I do not want to miss even one of them!"

"That is up to you. Since I am sure that you speak Greek, my sister is relying on you to teach her a few words which the people she will rule over will understand."

"I will do that! I promise you I will do that!"

The Duke climbed back into his carriage.

Valona and her mother waved him goodbye until he was out of sight.

The Duke leant back on the comfortable seat with a sigh of satisfaction.

He had been so afraid that his sister would refuse to go and then that the Queen would not allow the Marquis to represent her and travel with them.

And finally that he would be unable to find another Lady-in-Waiting.

Now all these difficulties had been solved.

He could only hope that the voyage would turn out as smooth and pleasant as it appeared at the moment.

Then he remembered that his dear sister Rose was to marry the elderly King when they arrived.

And that was the real hurdle at the end of the race.

He could only hope – almost against hope – that it would not be insurmountable.

CHAPTER TWO

The Duke had left them and Princess Louise talked excitedly for a long while about such a surprising offer and of what had been planned for her daughter.

Now Valona knew what she must do.

She waited until her mother had gone upstairs and then she slipped out of the house and ran over to one of the other houses at Hampton Court where she was welcomed as a frequent visitor.

Sir Mortimer Melgrave was a distinguished elderly diplomat who had served Great Britain well.

He had ended up as British Ambassador to Spain after serving in many different European Capitals where he was always spoken of as being 'the perfect diplomat.'

He was now getting on for eighty.

The Queen had presented him with one of the very best of the Grace and Favour houses – it was a particularly pleasant one because it had a large garden.

As the Princess and Valona were not so privileged, he invited them to come and sit in his garden at any time.

He had made it look very attractive, but Valona had other reasons for visiting him.

Because she was intensely interested in the places Sir Mortimer had lived in as a diplomat, he had told her that one day she must travel around the world.

"It is what I would like to do more than anything else," Valona told him fervently.

Sir Mortimer smiled.

"Then you will have to marry a rich man!"

She laughed.

"If we go on living here, as seems more than likely, it is doubtful I will ever find a man to dance with, let alone marry!"

Sir Mortimer knew that this was true and thought it rather pathetic.

It would have been so easy for the Queen to invite Princess Louise and Valona to some of her many parties at Windsor Castle and he felt too that the Princess's relatives were most remiss in taking no interest in her.

Princess Louise was too modest and retiring to push herself forward, but by now she was becoming increasingly worried about Valona.

She was now nearly old enough to be a *debutante*, but she would be invited to none of the parties to which she was entitled.

Valona knocked on the front door of Sir Mortimer's house and it was opened by his elderly servant.

"It's so nice to see Your Highness," he greeted her. "The Master be in the garden."

Valona smiled at him and ran straight through the small house into the garden behind it.

Sir Mortimer was sitting in the shade of a tree.

He had always been a very good-looking man and his looks had certainly been a great help to his career.

He was still most handsome in his old age and he was not at all bald, but his hair was white. His eyes, except for reading when he wore spectacles, were keen and bright.

Valona ran across the grass towards him.

He thought how lovely she was and how graceful.

"It is so nice to see you, Valona," he welcomed her. "You must forgive me for not getting up."

This was something he would always say to her in his usual courtly manner.

Valona sat down beside him on the wooden bench and slipped her arm through his.

"*What* do you think has happened?" she breathed.

"I can tell by your voice it is something exciting," replied Sir Mortimer.

"So exciting that I cannot believe it is true."

"Tell me," he begged.

"We saw the Duke of Inchcombe when we were at a funeral the other day and he has just called to see us."

Sir Mortimer looked surprised.

"For any particular reason?"

"A very important reason. He has asked me to take on the position of Lady-in-Waiting to his sister, Lady Rose, who is going to Larissa to marry the King."

"*Marry the King*! I should have thought he was far too old for His Grace's sister."

"He is very much too old," agreed Valona, "but the Russians are threatening to infiltrate into Larissa. As you know, the best way that Queen Victoria can stop them is to provide the King with an English bride related to her."

Sir Mortimer nodded his head.

"Of course, of course! Her Majesty is quite right. It is the one thing which will stop the Russians taking over every Balkan country, which is what they intend to do."

"What is so exciting is that I am to travel there with her and, of course, I want you to tell me all about Larissa. I remember you told me you had been in our Embassy once in Sofia."

"That is right, Valona, I was young at the time, but I well remember visiting Larissa on several occasions and thought it was a very pretty country."

"You must tell me all about it, please, and teach me a little of the language."

Sir Mortimer smiled.

"You will not have difficulty in that. Your Greek is good and Larissa has a great deal of Greek in its language, besides Serbian and a little, although only a little of what is original to them."

"We shall have to hurry," urged Valona, "because we leave in nine days time."

"Nine days!" cried Sir Mortimer. "Things must be worse in Larissa than I have heard."

"Apparently it is very serious, so please, please, Sir Mortimer, do help me to learn the language so that I can at least make myself understood to His Majesty."

"I would expect the King will speak a little English, but you should have plenty of time on the ship taking you there."

"The Duke told my Mama that we will be sailing to Larissa in a battleship and that too is so thrilling."

"I agree with you, but however exciting the voyage is, you will have to work hard, my dear, so as to be able to impress the people of Larissa when you arrive."

"I will try very hard. I feel so lucky it is one of the languages you know. It could easily have been a country such as China or even Japan, where I would not be able to speak a word."

"I do know a little Japanese!" smiled Sir Mortimer.

Then before Valona could say anything, he added,

"Now if you are going to any Balkan country, it is very important that you should be able to shoot."

Valona looked at him in surprise.

"You think I might be attacked?"

"One never knows and as I have told you so often when you talk about traversing the world, a woman should always be able to protect herself."

For that reason and also because it amused him, he had taught Valona to shoot several months previously.

He had placed a target at the end of his garden and made her try to hit the bull's-eye at the longest possible range.

When Princess Louise was told what her daughter was doing, she had smiled.

"I cannot believe, my dearest, it will ever come in useful, but I am certain your father, if he was alive, would have thought it a good idea. He was always determined that I should be able to defend myself in an emergency, but I am glad to say one never came."

"You did not have to shoot during the revolution in Piracus?" Valona had asked her.

Her mother had shaken her head.

"Your dear father rushed you and me to safety, but bravely he went back to see if there were any other women and children to save."

"And then the awful revolutionaries wounded him," murmured Valona.

"He was rescued by one of our loyal servants. All the others at the Palace were either killed or imprisoned."

There was always deep pain in the Princess's voice when she talked about what had happened in her husband's country.

Valona did not pursue the conversation.

She enjoyed learning to shoot with Sir Mortimer.

She had only finished with her shooting lessons as she had become really proficient and there were so many other subjects to talk to him about.

Now Sir Mortimer rose slowly to his feet.

"Where are you going?" Valona asked him.

"I am going to look amongst my books to find if I have any printed in Larissian. I am sure I have one or two, and you must read them word for word when I am not with you."

"I was sure that you could help me," sighed Valona, slipping her hand into his. "When shall I come to you for my lessons? Mama and I will be very busy in buying my new clothes."

Valona had not exaggerated in the least, as during the next week she hardly had time to breathe.

She and the Princess drove up to London every day soon after breakfast to visit the shops and then when they had chosen what they wanted, there were endless fittings.

There was also a great number of small items which were essential but easily overlooked.

After six days the spare room in their house, which was not very big, seemed to be filled from floor to ceiling.

There were not only the beautiful dresses that made Valona gasp, because they were so incredibly lovely, but there were the matching hats which went with them.

As well as the array of shoes, gloves, petticoats and nightgowns, there were dozens of other accessories which the Princess ticked off on her list as they bought them.

Valona wanted to please Sir Mortimer as well as herself, so every afternoon as soon as they returned from shopping, she went over to his house to have lessons in the language of Larissa.

Every night before she fell asleep she read a little of the two books he had given her written in Larissian.

One was rather dull as it was a very basic technical description of the country and the minerals in it.

The other book was a romantic novel which was far easier and she enjoyed the story.

She found it was so easy to remember the words of love the hero spoke to the heroine.

She was given several more shooting lessons at the weekend, when it was impossible to go to London because all the shops were closed.

Sir Mortimer found that, although she had not been practising for several months, she had not forgotten any of his instructions.

In fact, as he told her, she used her revolver like a professional and he was very proud of his pupil.

When she hit the bull's-eye the fifth time out of six, he said that he doubted if he could teach her any more.

He only hoped that she would not have to use the revolver to defend herself.

"Are you really allowing me to take the revolver?" Valona enquired. "I am certain that Mama would think it a waste of money for me to buy one and I promise you I will take great care of yours and give it back to you as soon as I come home."

"I doubt if I shall need to defend myself very often here," smiled Sir Mortimer. "But one just never knows in foreign countries, especially when the enemy is *Russian*."

His voice was very serious as he added quietly,

"Trust no one and be careful with whom you make friends."

"I just cannot believe, Sir Mortimer, that I shall be in any danger, but I do hope they will be very careful with Lady Rose. If the Russians want to invade or take over a country, they will not want its King to marry and have a family."

Sir Mortimer smiled.

"He has been married already and has a son."

Valona looked surprised.

"I believed that the most important reason for his marriage was that there was no one to become King when he dies."

"I think you will find the real reason for him getting married is to have the Union Jack flying over Larissa," Sir Mortimer replied. "I think it is very brave of Lady Rose, who is so very young, to marry a man so that she can save his country for him."

"How old is the King?" Valona wanted to know.

"Fifty-five – fifty-six, somewhere about there."

Valona gave a cry of horror.

"But Lady Rose is not much older than me! I think Mama said she is only nearing twenty."

"Royal marriages are normally made for a political reason and it is not hard to find a very good reason for the King of Larissa to take an English wife."

"Do you really think the Russians are trying to take over his country?"

"His Majesty must be convinced of it, or he would not have asked for Queen Victoria's help in finding him an English wife."

Valona told her mother what Sir Mortimer had said and she agreed that it was very hard luck on Lady Rose.

"You must do your very best to make her happy, my dearest," she urged Valona. "I think it is most patriotic of her to agree to anything so difficult, even if Her Majesty has pressured her into doing so."

"I will try and help her in every way I can not to feel homesick, Mama," Valona promised.

The Princess bent and kissed her daughter.

"I am sure you will do so, my dearest, but I do not want you to stay away too long."

"I will only stay until Lady Rose is well settled in and takes on a Lady-in-Waiting who will enjoy being with her. I expect that she is learning to speak Larissian, but she may not be too good at languages."

"Which you are, my dear Valona, and is yet another excellent reason why you should go to Larissa with Lady Rose, even though I shall miss you terribly."

"And I shall miss you, Mama. I do wish you could come too."

Her mother held up her hands.

"No, no, I have done enough travelling in my life. I am quite content to stay put here in this house, even though it will be so lonely without you and your father."

Valona felt worried about her mother, but she was delighted the next day when they came back from shopping to find there was a letter for the Princess from the Duke's mother, the Dowager Duchess.

She invited her, as soon as Valona had left England with Lady Rose, to come and stay at Combe Hall.

She was still living in the ancestral home that now belonged to her son, the Duke, and, as he had no wife, she was, as she explained, still the chatelaine of Combe Hall.

The Duchess had written,

"*I find it so sad that we have seen so little of each other these past years.*

But I feel we shall have so much to talk about if you come for a nice long stay after our daughters have set out for Larissa.

Please let me know when I can expect you.

I am sure a lot of the family whom you have not yet met will be delighted to make your acquaintance."

"That is a very lovely letter, Mama, and now I shall feel a lot happier at leaving you. I am sure if you stay with the Dowager Duchess you will soon be invited by all the other relatives. In fact when I come home, I doubt if you will have any time for me at all!"

The Princess laughed.

"I shall always have time for you, my dearest, but it is very kind of the Duchess and I shall look forward to my stay with her."

Because her mother's clothes were becoming very shabby, Valona had insisted on buying a few new dresses for her at the same time as she was obtaining her own.

"The Duke said he would pay for yours, not mine," her mother protested.

"I am quite certain he would be delighted for you to have two or three gowns, Mama, and if you are going to be difficult about it, I shall refuse to have the dresses we have ordered today."

Princess Louise took much persuading, but finally she gave in.

She was well aware how rich the Duke was and she knew she would feel uncomfortable looking a dowdy poor relation at the parties the Dowager Duchess would give at Combe Hall.

*

The days seemed to flash by.

Valona finally said her farewells to Sir Mortimer.

"I have read your books from cover to cover," she told him, "and thank you so much for lending them to me."

"I have cleaned my revolver and it is now ready for you, Valona, and a good supply of bullets, although again I hope you will not need them."

"I hope not too, but I am sure I am right in thinking

one should always be prepared."

She was remembering as she spoke what her father had often said,

"It was largely owing to lack of preparation and in some ways sheer carelessness on the part of my people that the revolution in Piracus was so successful."

There had been no resistance and they had been so lucky to have been able to escape.

All the revolutionaries had despised the Piracusian Army and had not expected the Prince to oppose them in any effective way.

Valona packed the revolver in one of her trunks and sent up a prayer as she did so that it would not be needed.

'I am sure that as there has been so much trouble in the Balkans already,' she mused confidently, 'that Larissa, as well as requesting protection from Great Britain, will be making some effort to protect itself.'

The Duke had arranged everything in minute detail and would send one of his carriages to collect Valona and her mother.

He had explained in his letter they were to meet at Combe House in Park Lane.

The battleship would be waiting in the Thames near the House of Commons.

For Valona it was all wildly exciting.

She was half afraid when she went to bed the night before that something would happen to prevent her leaving.

When the morning came, the carriage arrived soon after breakfast.

All Valona's luggage was piled into it and she and her mother drove off in considerable style waving goodbye to their elderly servant.

"You have explained to me, Mama," said Valona as the horses drove through Windsor, "exactly what my duties are as a Lady-in-Waiting, but surely I shall not be the only one."

"I think you are the only English one, my dearest. When she becomes Queen of Larissa, Lady Rose will be expected to have a number of Larissian ladies in attendance upon her. They might consider it to be offensive if she had more than one of her own nationality."

"Oh, I see what you mean. So I shall not have to be on duty all the time."

"I expect that you will sometimes have time to read a book or go for a good long walk in the garden. But in my experience of Royal households, there is always such a lot of protocol and bowing and curtsying that one never has a moment to oneself!"

"I expect I shall be able to steal some moments and I only hope they have a library. I have packed a number of books, but I could not bear having nothing to read."

"I should speak to the Duke before you reach your destination," her mother advised. "I expect, because he is such a charming young man, he will contrive some way of helping you."

"I hope so," Valona agreed doubtfully. "As well as books I shall want horses to ride."

The Princess wondered if her daughter was asking too much, but at the same time she knew herself how dull and boring a Royal Court could be, especially when there was nothing in particular happening.

"As everything has been done in such a hurry," she said, "because of the death of the Lady-in-Waiting whose place you are taking, I am sure if you really want to come home soon, the Duke and I will be able to find someone to replace you."

"That is a consolation for me, but I am really a little scared of departing into the unknown and having nothing to do."

The Princess chuckled.

"You will find plenty to do, my dearest, and I look forward to your letters telling me you are overworked and longing to come home for a rest!"

Valona laughed as she was meant to and then she kissed her mother on the cheek.

"I do love you, Mama. We have always managed to laugh however difficult things have been."

The Princess knew that their lives had really been a tremendous effort, especially after the loss of her husband.

At the same time Valona was just so full of life and energy.

It had always been easy for them to find something interesting to talk about or do, however little money they had.

When they arrived in Park Lane, Valona was very impressed by Combe House, which stood by itself with a large garden behind it.

The rooms seemed to her enormous after their tiny spaces at Hampton Court and all the Duke's magnificent pictures and furniture made Valona gasp.

'This is the way my dear Mama should be living,' she mused to herself. 'Only it should be a Palace.'

The Duke was waiting for them both in the drawing room with his sister, Lady Rose.

She was very pretty, Valona thought, and she took a liking to her from the moment Lady Rose thanked her for agreeing to come with her as Lady-in-Waiting.

"I think it is angelic of you," she said. "It would be terrible if I had to be accompanied by some fussy old body, who never stopped telling me everything I did was wrong

34

or someone who talked so much that I never got a word in edgeways!"

Valona giggled.

"I assure you that I shall never do either of those things."

There was, however, little time to talk and the Duke kept saying they should go aboard.

Finally Valona said farewell to her mother and for a moment there was a suspicion of tears in the eyes of both of them.

"Take care of yourself, darling Mama, and if you need me, I promise I will come back at once."

"I just want you to enjoy yourself and be a great success, my dearest."

She kissed her daughter again and then she turned away so that she should not see the tears in her eyes.

They drove off and the Duke sat beside his sister with Valona on the other side of them.

As she said goodbye, Princess Louise did think that as Valona was so beautiful the Duke might be attracted to her.

Stranger things could happen in life, although more frequently in books, but she was aware that the Duke had looked at Valona admiringly and with satisfaction.

"Your daughter is very lovely," he had said to her in an aside.

"I cannot tell you how grateful we are to you for the lovely clothes you have given her," added Princess Louise.

"Valona will certainly carry the flag admirably."

Princess Louise sighed.

"That is true, but she is very young and it is a great responsibility for a girl of that age."

"Rose will look after her very well," the Duke told her confidently, "so you are not to worry."

She watched the carriage until it was out of sight as she was pondering somewhat wistfully how much she was going to miss Valona.

*

Lady Rose was rather quiet on the way to join the battleship.

Her brother was well aware why.

She was terrified that at the last moment something would prevent the Marquis from joining them.

He realised only too well how crafty his sister had been in pushing him into suggesting to the Queen that she should appoint the Marquis as her representative to Larissa.

He was pleased also that they had managed to avoid having to take a member of the Larissian Court with them.

The Marquis had made it clear that it would take too long to wait for them to return from Larissa to England so they had next suggested that the Larissians might send a diplomat from Paris or Berlin.

The Marquis had then made a clever excuse that the battleship was not in the least commodious enough for too many guests, and it would be more pleasant for the English party to be free of pomp and ceremony until they actually reached Larissa.

They were piped aboard the battleship.

After shaking hands with the Captain and his fellow Officers, they went below.

As was usual the Captain had given up his sleeping cabin as well as his day cabin to the most important guest aboard – Lady Rose.

As this battleship had been responsible for carrying Royalty on other State occasions, it was well furnished and comfortable.

When they were alone after a Steward had brought

36

them coffee, tea and sandwiches, the Duke turned to speak to the Marquis,

"I congratulate you, Gerald. I quite expected at the last moment we should have some dreary old Statesman or retired diplomat coming with us."

"We very nearly had a whole tribe of them," replied the Marquis. "But now we are, thank Heaven, on our own. So let's try to forget for a few moments that *all good things come to an end.*"

He was looking at Lady Rose as he spoke and the expression in her eyes surprised Valona.

She thought the Marquis looked very handsome as he came aboard.

She found it rather surprising that there was not an older lady to accompany them, as her mother had expected there to be a husband and wife from the Palace entourage in Larissa and that they would be present to welcome them officially on behalf of the King.

The Marquis glanced over his shoulder in order to make sure the door was closed and no one was listening.

"What I have arranged, Arthur, is for messages to be sent to me at every port at which we call."

"Are we calling at any ports?" asked the Duke. "It is the first I have heard of it."

"That is what I have arranged and I thought it rather bright of me. It will make the voyage take longer naturally and I am certain that Valona, if no one else, would like to have a look at Gibraltar, Marseilles, Naples and Athens."

"I would love it," cried Valona, before anyone else could speak. "All my life I have always longed to visit all those places. Do you think we could possibly stop, if only for a few minutes, in Venice?"

"I have to admit I missed that one out," the Marquis

laughed, "but it will certainly have to be included!"

He put out his hand towards Lady Rose.

"Tell me I have been clever."

"Very clever," she replied in a soft voice.

They were looking deeply into each other's eyes.

And it suddenly struck Valona as extraordinary, but it seemed that they might be in love with each other.

'I must be imagining it,' she scolded herself.

At the same time, although she knew nothing about love, she was almost sure that it was what those two people were feeling.

Now they were all on board and the ship's engines were turning.

H.M.S. Victorious was starting to move slowly and sedately up the centre of the River Thames.

"I think that we should go on deck now," the Duke suggested to Valona. "You will have a very good view of the Houses of Parliament before we move down the river."

She followed him eagerly.

Out on deck he pointed out the important sights as they passed them.

Next she realised that Lady Rose and the Marquis had not come with them.

She sighed, as it was thrilling to be on a battleship and to be seeing London from an entirely new and different angle.

She thought it was such a pity that Lady Rose was missing it.

However, she was very content to be with the Duke who she found knew a great deal about history.

He told her about the building of London and how it had changed down the centuries.

"I do wish Mama could see what you are showing me now!" exclaimed Valona.

"I tell you what we will do. When we come back from Larissa, perhaps in six months or even a year's time, we will take your mother in my yacht down the Thames as we are proceeding now."

Valona clasped her hands together.

"What a wonderful idea! You are so kind to us and Mama would enjoy it all so much."

"You are not to worry about her. I am sure she will be quite happy staying with my mother and the gardens are looking at their best at this time of the year."

"I know that you must have asked your mother to invite Mama to Combe House, Cousin Arthur, and I am so very grateful to you. Otherwise I would have been worried that she would be lonely without me."

"I had thought about it, Valona, and I am only so ashamed as one of the family that we have neglected your dear mother for so long. It slipped my mind that we were related and now you must help me make up for it."

"I am only too willing to do whatever you want and please say that you like my dress and hat, all of which you paid for."

The Duke chuckled.

"I can see that like all women you would like to be flattered. Actually I am not flattering you, but telling you the truth when I say that you are exactly the right person to impress the Russians that the British are all powerful!"

Valona smiled.

"I don't think I am capable of that, but at least no one will patronise me because I look threadbare."

"It is something which will never occur again," the

Duke promised. "I have already apologised that you have been neglected."

"We have been extremely happy at Hampton Court. There are such kind people living there and they all came yesterday afternoon to wish me goodbye and said such nice things about me to my Mama that I was almost sorry to be leaving."

"And what do you feel about it now?"

"This is the most fantastic thing I have ever done," answered Valona, "even in my dreams."

"I saw you looking very animated when my friend the Marquis told us we were stopping at a number of ports on our way to Larissa, so I would imagine that you long to be a traveller."

"So far I have only been able to travel in my mind and through the books I have read. Now I am really going to see the great Rock of Gibraltar and the canals of Venice! I feel sure that once again I am dreaming!"

"I only hope you will not be disappointed, Valona. If one sets one's expectations too high, there is always the chance that you wish the reality could have been a little bit better."

Valona laughed.

"Now you are being cynical. I am sure that none of us have any doubts that this magical ship will carry us into an enchanted fairyland!"

The Duke was silent for a minute before he replied,

"That is what we hope Larissa will be like after we have arrived there. Despite what Gerald desires, we must not linger too long on the voyage."

"Why do you say that?"

The Duke hesitated for just a moment as he thought it might be mistake to tell her the truth and then he said,

"I think, Valona, you are old enough to understand the Russian intentions in the Balkans and it will not please them that the King of Larissa is marrying again, although he is no longer a young man, and above all to an English bride related to Queen Victoria."

"He already has a son, I hear."

"One child is not enough for a safe dynasty."

The Duke spoke in a low voice almost as if he was talking to himself.

"If Larissa is really in such danger," Valona asked him, "why do you allow your sister to go there?"

The Duke smiled a little wryly.

"It is what the Queen desires and it is very difficult to oppose Her Majesty when she has made up her mind!"

"I appreciate that and I was rather frightened that she might send for me and, when she had seen me, decide that I was too young."

The Duke laughed.

"You must be clairvoyant. That is just what I was scared of too. So in case the Queen said that she wanted to see you first, I quickly told her that you were away from home visiting one of your relatives.

"That was a lie!"

"A white lie, shall we say, Valona, but I think if she had seen you, she might well have insisted on Rose being accompanied by some aged crone who would have found fault with everything we did from the moment we left."

"That would have been dreadful. And thank you, thank you, Cousin Arthur, for being so clever even if it was a lie."

"A white lie," insisted the Duke, "and it is certainly permissible if it is helping someone else."

As they steamed past the ancient Tower of London

and then the dockyards, the Duke told Valona something of their long and interesting history.

A little later it was time for luncheon, so they went down to the Saloon.

As they entered Valona could see that the Marquis and Lady Rose were deep in conversation with each other.

They did not seem to be particularly happy and he was holding her hand in his.

It then struck Valona that perhaps the Marquis had wanted to marry Lady Rose, and she had been obliged to refuse him because she was to marry the King.

'If it was me,' Valona thought, 'and I was in love with anyone half as good-looking as the Marquis, I would refuse the King whatever Her Majesty might say about it!'

After luncheon Lady Rose told Valona that she was going to rest and did not wish to be disturbed.

"I have not brought a lady's maid with me, so I do hope you will help me later with my gown."

"Of course I will," replied Valona.

Lady Rose continued,

"My brother's valet, who has been with us since I was a little girl, is so clever at packing and unpacking, it would be such a nuisance to have a lady's maid on board as well, who anyway would doubtless be seasick!"

She did not say anything else, but walked into the Captain's cabin and closed the door.

Valona had no wish to lie down when she might be on deck, so she ran up the companionway.

At the top she almost bumped into the Marquis who was just going down the stairs.

"If you are looking for Arthur," he said, "you will find him somewhere on deck or he might be on the bridge with the Captain."

"Thank you," Valona replied.

The Marquis then hurried down the companionway.

She thought it a little strange that he should wish to be below – as he was a man he was not likely to be tired like Lady Rose.

On deck the sun was shining and Valona thought that any man would want to be out in the fresh air.

In a short time there would be a touch of salt in the air blowing in from the sea.

'It's all so wonderful,' she told herself, 'and I have no wish to miss anything. I will tell Mama about it when I write to her.'

She went out on deck and saw the Duke leaning over the rails.

When she joined him, he smiled at her.

"I suppose you would like to see us move into the Channel."

"I want to see everything and miss nothing!"

"I will try to help you do just that," said the Duke.

"You are so kind," answered Valona. "Nothing as fabulous as this has ever happened in my life before."

She was obviously so thrilled with everything and looked so lovely that the Duke smiled at her.

However he knew that every mile they steamed on made his sister more miserable.

And it was the same for the Marquis.

There was nothing he could do to help them.

At least they would be able to be together until they reached Larissa.

It seemed cruel that it was all they would have to remember for the rest of their lives.

Yet he supposed it was better than nothing.

"You are looking worried, Cousin Arthur," Valona piped up unexpectedly. "Have I said something wrong?"

"No, of course not. I was just reflecting that very few people are as happy as you are at this moment. I wish we could wave a magic wand and give happiness, if not to the whole world, at least to those we love."

"It would be marvellous, if we could do it! When Mama was so unhappy after my Papa died, I felt helpless because I could not bring him back to life."

"I can understand."

"Mama was very brave," said Valona, "because she believed that Papa, although he was no longer with us, was looking after and protecting us. Perhaps it is all due to him that I am having this superb treat."

"I do hope everything you do in life will be equally wonderful for you, but I expect like everyone else we will have our ups and downs and setbacks, however hard we try to avoid them."

"Of course we will, but when we manage all on our own, or perhaps with the help of those we cannot see, to be given such a unique opportunity as I have been given, it is the magical happiness which we seek and when we have found it, we must hold on to it very very tightly."

"You are so right," he agreed. "Perhaps in that way we shall miss very little and gain a great deal."

He was thinking as he spoke that it was impossible for Rose and Gerald and he could only hope that the short time they were now together would be some compensation.

CHAPTER THREE

They reached Gibraltar without suffering too much from a rough sea in the Bay of Biscay.

Valona was quite right in thinking she would not be seasick.

She managed to spend a great deal of time on deck watching majestic waves break over the ship's bow and did not mind occasionally being sprayed herself.

Lady Rose stayed mostly down below.

The second day they were out, Valona suggested,

"You know, Rose, it is time you must start learning the language of Larissa, because you will be asked to make a speech as soon as you arrive."

"Why should I have to do that?" she asked rather disagreeably.

"Mama told me that when Royal persons arrive in a foreign country, they are always met by the Prime Minister and Members of the Cabinet. After they bid you welcome, you are expected to reply in their language."

"Well, it had better be short, otherwise I shall not remember what I am to say!"

Valona had already written down a little speech for Lady Rose to make.

She tried to teach it to her word by word, but she had the feeling that Lady Rose was not listening, but was anxious to get away from her.

The next day Valona tried once again, but she flatly refused.

Then she realised it was because she wanted to be with the Marquis – they spent the afternoon sitting close together in a shady part of the ship, where they could not be seen by the crew.

Valona sensed it was no use trying to disturb them and because the Duke was afraid that was what she might do, he challenged her to a game of deck tennis.

Valona had never played it before, but she picked it up quickly and although the Duke won easily, she managed to make him fight for it.

Dinner was a quiet meal with the Duke doing most of the talking.

The Marquis and Rose just gazed at each other.

Valona by this time was absolutely convinced that they were in love and she felt that the whole situation must be most difficult for them.

She was somewhat worried in case she did anything wrong and so she said to the Duke the next day when they were alone,

"I have been attempting to encourage Rose to learn a short speech for when she arrives at Larissa, but she does not seem at all interested. I just feel that she is unhappy at having to marry the King."

"Of course, she is unhappy, Valona, but the Queen made it almost a command. In any case it is hopeless for Rose to stay on in England without being able to see my friend Gerald."

Valona thought that this was a strange thing to say.

She merely glanced at the Duke questioningly and he explained,

"You realise by now that they are in love with each

other and it is impossible for them to hide it. But there is nothing they can do."

"Because the Marquis is married?" Valona asked in a low voice.

"If you know that fact, I suppose whoever told you added the information that his wife is incurably mad!"

Valona looked startled.

Her mother had said that the Marquis was married, but she had certainly not added that information about his wife.

There was a silence before Valona remarked,

"It must be very sad for him – "

"It is a terrible tragedy. She was very beautiful and apparently charming in every possible way. No one told him that she had certain seizures and although he has consulted dozens of doctors, they have been able to do nothing for her."

Valona thought it was the most dreadful story.

"I am sorry, so very very sorry. Of course, Rose does not want to leave him and every one else she loves."

"You must help her if you can," urged the Duke.

"Of course I will. She is so sweet and I want her to be happy, but if *you* cannot do anything, who can?"

"I suppose, Valona, that if Gerald and Rose were of little importance, they could run away together and would soon be forgotten, but they come from powerful families, who would both suffer from the scandal, and if Rose had children they would not have a name."

Valona felt it was the saddest situation that anyone could find themselves in.

She was thus more attentive and gentler with Lady Rose than she had been before.

It was as she was fastening her gown before dinner that Rose blurted out,

"I think you realise, Valona, how unhappy I am."

"Your brother has told me," she replied, "and I am so very sorry for you."

"I am sorry for myself, but there is nothing I can do and it would be wicked to drag Gerald's name through the mud."

"Of course it would," agreed Valona. "And I shall pray every single night when I say my prayers that perhaps one day you will be able to be together."

Lady Rose did not answer.

Valona realised she was thinking it was impossible for there to be any way out of their misery.

Quite suddenly Lady Rose put her hands up to her eyes.

"I just cannot bear it," she moaned. "I really think I would rather die than be married to another man, knowing I can never see my darling Gerald again."

There was a painful pause before she added,

"I think I will kill myself. I believe drowning is not too unpleasant."

"Suppose you did so," replied Valona, "and then by some miracle the Marquis became free. Can you imagine what he would feel?"

Lady Rose took her hands from her face.

Her tears had overflowed down her cheeks and she looked very pathetic.

"How can there be any chance of that?" she asked. "Gerald's wife is only twenty-three and the doctors say she could live until she is sixty or seventy."

"You never know, Rose, something might happen,

but in any case it would be wicked to take your own life. Remember, if you are suffering, I am sure that the Marquis is suffering too."

"He is," agreed Lady Rose, "and it breaks my heart when he tells me how much he loves me whilst I know we can never be together."

"I do think, Rose, that you are giving in too easily. You must believe that things will come right. Not at once, but maybe at some point in the years ahead. Then it would be terrible for you both if, when you could be together, one of you was missing."

Lady Rose gave a little sob.

"I understand exactly what you are saying to me. I only wish I could see even one small ray of sunshine in the darkness ahead."

"But it is there! I am sure it is there."

Valona was silent for a moment and then added,

"Mama told me that, as I was born under a lucky star, the people in Papa's country believed I had a magic eye. They claimed that when I was older I would be able to tell fortunes."

Lady Rose was listening and Valona went on,

"Mama said they used to touch my pram hoping it would bring them luck and, when everyone was so terrified at the time of the revolution, I was quite certain that Papa, Mama and I would be able to escape."

"And with your magic eye you can see that Gerald and I will be together?"

"I am sure in my heart that one day, I have no idea when, your love will unite you both and that you will be happy."

"I want to believe you," groaned Lady Rose. "God knows I want to believe you."

"Then you must pray every night for what you want as my Mama taught me to do, and your Guardian Angel, or perhaps even your very special star in the sky, will bring you happiness."

"I will tell Gerald what you have said, although he will doubtless pooh-pooh the idea, I do know he too would love to believe you are telling the truth."

"I am telling you something that I sincerely believe is the truth, Rose, and I am quite certain it will all come true, although you may have to wait a little while."

"Every day spent without my Gerald will seem like an eternity. But you have made me feel happier and for the moment I promise you I will not drown myself."

"You are certainly not to do anything so wicked or even think about it," Valona scolded her.

The two girls were smiling as they walked into the Saloon for dinner.

The Marquis jumped up from his chair and ran to Lady Rose's side and exclaimed,

"You are looking happy. What has happened?"

"I will tell you all about it later," she answered him mysteriously.

Dinner seemed more amusing that night than it had been on previous nights.

When they went to bed, Valona thought it had been the happiest evening they had yet spent together.

She was feeling particularly excited because they were stopping at Gibraltar tomorrow and she so wanted to visit the Rock.

The Duke had promised he would take her ashore and she would see the famous monkeys.

She felt so glad that they were not going to Larissa without stopping en route.

"Was there anything waiting for you at Government House?" the Duke asked the Marquis when he returned on board after their short stop in Gibraltar.

The Marquis shook his head.

"Nothing of any importance except that my trainer have entered one of my horses in the big race at Epsom this afternoon."

"Do you think it will win?" the Duke enquired.

"It might do."

"It's a pity you are not there to see him first past the winning post."

The Marquis smiled.

"I would rather be here at the moment," he replied emphatically and walked away.

The sun was shining brightly and the Mediterranean was blue and Valona thought it was very beautiful.

The battleship did not take long to reach Marseilles and again the Marquis set off to visit the British Consulate.

The Duke, however, told Valona that there was no point in going ashore as there was very little to see.

"Just a busy French commercial town," he told her, "and you can do all the sightseeing you could ever desire when we reach Naples and then on to Venice."

"I am longing to see the canals," said Valona, "and I have read the complete history of Venice and, of course, seen pictures of it."

"I just hope you will not be too disappointed and I have often found myself, when I have been travelling, that the description of the place is often far more exciting than the place itself."

"I think that sounds rather blasé. Perhaps you have

been spoilt by travelling to too many Cities. I really cannot believe that there is not something new and exciting to see in every foreign town."

The Duke chortled.

"As you are so much of an optimist, I will merely wish you luck and not try to disillusion you, Valona."

"I don't think I shall be disillusioned in any way," she persisted. "But books always pick out the very best of the sights and historic buildings to write up, and sometimes they ignore special little gems of even greater interest than the major attractions."

The Duke laughed and continued to tease her.

At the same time he felt it was quite extraordinary that this young girl, having no experience of the world, had worked out such truths for herself.

He had noticed at dinner she always had something unusual and intelligent to contribute to the conversation.

In fact, he said to himself, she is almost too good to be true!

'She looks,' he ruminated, 'just as beautiful as she ought to be in the clothes I have provided for her!'

He liked the unselfconscious way that Valona had thanked him and she politely asked his opinion about every new gown she put on.

"Mama hesitated over this one," she had remarked this morning when she came up on deck. "She thought any colour would be a little too bright for England, but I hope you will think this is just right for the Mediterranean."

"You look very lovely in it," commented the Duke.

Valona gave a little skip of delight.

"That is exactly what I want to hear and I will write and tell Mama what you have said."

The Duke thought when they returned to England he would organise one of his relations to introduce Valona to London Society.

She would certainly shine at all the balls that took place every night in the Season.

He would also ensure that she and her mother were invited when there was a ball or some particularly grand occasion at Windsor Castle.

'Valona will enjoy every moment of it all,' he told himself. 'She has managed to cheer up Rose a little today, for which I am very grateful.'

That night when the girls retired to bed, Lady Rose asked Valona,

"You are praying for me to your special star?"

"Yes, I am, Rose, but you must pray to your star as well. I strongly suspect it does not work for anyone else."

She spoke very seriously and so obviously believed in every word she was saying that Lady Rose did what she was told.

When she repeated to the Marquis what Valona had told her, he said,

"Now I think of it, I have heard that is one of the beliefs of the people of Piracus, but it didn't do much good for the poor Prince. The throne rather was shaky before he inherited it and I doubt if that country will ever again have a Royal Ruler."

"Their star did not look after them properly," Lady Rose responded.

"Perhaps they were a bit remiss with their prayers and we can only hope, my darling one, that your star will listen to you."

As there was nothing more to say, he kissed Lady Rose tenderly.

And for a moment they were both transported into a special Heaven of their own.

*

The next port of call was Naples.

Despite its poverty Valona thought how attractive the City was.

The others became a little interested as well and the Duke took them to Pompeii.

Valona was shocked to see how cruelly the people living there at the time had suffered and yet she found the ruins entrancing – so much still remained of what had once been a great City.

They drove back along narrow roads with the sea on one side of them.

Valona slipped her hand into the Duke's.

"I never thought the day would come when I would see Pompeii," she sighed. "I have read about it and have seen pictures of it, but nothing can be the same as seeing it for myself."

"There is a great deal more of the world to see, and I think it would be a good idea that at the end of your visit you should write a guide book telling people like yourself, who have always stayed at home, the difference between what they read and what they would actually see."

"There are never going to be enough words in the English dictionary to describe it properly!"

The Duke laughed.

"I cannot believe that would stop you. I have come to the inevitable conclusion that you are a most determined young lady, who will doubtless end up instructing a whole lot of people what they should do whether they want it or not!"

Valona knew he was teasing her and laughed too.

"I will try not to be a dictator, Cousin Arthur, but at

the same time I do find myself seeing things, which could have been much better described in the books I have read about them."

The Duke threw up his hands in pretended horror.

"The one thing I am scared of is over-clever women who believe they are always right. Women should be soft, sweet, gentle and quiet."

Naturally Valona argued strenuously with him on this statement.

Their arguments on any subject always ended in the same way with them both laughing rather helplessly.

The Duke was very aware that the party travelling to Larissa would have been unbelievably gloomy if it had not been for Valona.

She even made Lady Rose laugh and smile as well as the men, as she always had something unusual to say.

She had already made friends with the Captain and many of the ordinary seamen of the crew.

The Duke observed that when she talked to them and enquired about their wives and families, the men never became over-familiar – they treated Valona with as much respect as they gave him.

He thought it so extraordinary after living the quiet life at Hampton Court.

Although she had received some instruction from various teachers, she had apparently learnt most about life from her books.

Yet she undoubtedly had the human touch.

'It must surely come from her father and mother,' the Duke mused. 'Equally it is most unusual in someone so young.'

He thought that even the Queen might be impressed with Valona. It would be amusing when she returned home to take Valona to Windsor Castle and hear afterwards what she thought of the Queen and her Court.

It was after they had sailed away from Naples that Valona became particularly excited.

"I think," she insisted, "from what I have read that Venice must be the most romantic City in the whole wide world."

To be argumentative the Duke challenged her,

"You will have to wait until you have visited some parts of India, China and Japan before you can make such a sweeping statement – incidentally the Pyramids of Egypt are not far away."

"Now you are being unkind to me, as you know I shall never have a chance of going to those places."

She paused for a moment before saying,

"Of course, I may be disappointed in Venice, but I cannot believe that will happen."

"The only answer is to see it, Valona, for yourself!"

*

They reached Venice the next morning and they all disembarked after breakfast.

They were carried by the battleship's skiff into the Grand Canal itself and stopped while the Duke engaged a gondola.

Venice was even lovelier and much more beautiful than Valona could ever have anticipated.

She was thrilled by the Piazza San Marco with its fluttering pigeons and sincerely impressed by the Doge's Palace with its carved heads of allegorical figures.

The Sansovino Library completed in 1591 made her want to spend a month in it.

Their gondola rowed them down the Grand Canal and Valona was strangely silent until the Duke asked,

"What has happened to you? After all that talk, are you disappointed at what you see before you?"

"I am just making sure that everything I am seeing is all true and will not disappear after a few seconds!"

They both laughed and she realised that they were managing to keep Lady Rose's spirits considerably higher than they usually were.

There were no messages waiting for the Marquis at the Consulate, however, they had already learnt when they were at Naples that his horse had been second in the race.

"What are you expecting to hear about at this port of call?" asked the Duke.

"Oh, nothing of importance. There is another race in which I have entered two of my horses on Saturday, but I don't expect either of them to win. It is just good practice for them."

"I would like you to have a look at my horses when I return to England," suggested the Duke, "and I hope you will come down to Newmarket with me."

He realised as he spoke that his sister gave a little quiver – she was very obviously thinking that while Gerald could do so, she would be far away.

He had not intended to be tactless and he quickly began to talk of something else.

At the same time he was very conscious that they were sailing nearer and nearer to Larissa and the dreadful moment would come when Rose and Gerald would have to say goodbye to each other for ever.

The Duke's family had urged him to find himself a bride time after time.

He did recognise that at some point in the future he would have to provide an heir to his illustrious title.

But what he had seen of Gerald and Rose's agony

made him feel that marriage was almost too much of a risk to take.

Supposing he did fall in love with some girl in the future and his marriage to her turned out to be as appalling for him as it was for Gerald.

The woman he would chose might not be mad, but she might be unfaithful.

Or after they had been married she might become in some way repulsive so that he could not bear to touch her.

There were so many things which might destroy a marriage.

It was, he determined, only love that could hold it together and make it the perfection that every man desired in his heart.

'I will definitely not marry until I absolutely have to,' the Duke resolved to himself firmly.

He thought with satisfaction of a certain charming and exceedingly attractive dancer, who would, he knew, be waiting eagerly for his return.

She was an amusing and delightful part of his life and yet if he had to give her up tomorrow, it would not break his heart – nor would it break hers.

There was too much at risk in marrying as Gerald had, believing he was deeply in love and totally convinced he would live happily ever after with his beautiful bride for the rest of their lives – and then came disaster.

'If that happened to me,' he pondered, 'I would find it impossible to go on living.'

His thoughts were all gloomy that night.

*

The next day they were steaming towards Athens and Valona had them all laughing again.

"Now you will be seeing the Goddesses of Ancient Greece," stated the Duke. "Both you and Rose will realise how inadequately you have managed to copy them!"

Before the two could protest, the Marquis added,

"On the contrary, Arthur, I think both the ladies we have with us are the personification of beauty. If there is any competition it is from Athene and Aphrodite who will have to look to their laurels and smarten *themselves* up!"

"Thank you! Thank you!" cried Lady Rose. "That was such a pretty speech and Valona and I want to believe you."

"You know you can believe everything I say about you," the Marquis murmured in a low voice.

She turned to smile at him and the words she was about to say died on her lips.

Again they were looking into each other's eyes.

The cabin seemed to vibrate with their love.

Valona was busy that evening looking amongst the books she had brought with her for the one on Greece, that she had borrowed from Sir Mortimer.

Naturally she had read it many times already.

She turned over the pages knowing that tomorrow she would be able to see some of the beauties of Greece.

She thought it must be the most exciting moment of her entire life.

Her mother had so often talked to her about Greece and her father's country was a part of it.

However Valona was more interested in Delphi and in the small Greek Islands, especially Delos where Apollo was born, besides all the other stories of Greece which she had read about and loved ever since she could remember.

'I shall see them! I shall really see them!' she told herself.

She thought that tomorrow would never come and it was hard to go to sleep.

She felt excitement rising in her breast.

Annoyingly it took longer to reach Greece than she had expected and it was almost dark when they eventually moved into Piraeus, the Port of Athens.

"I suppose it's too late to go ashore now," she said wistfully to the Duke.

"Much too late," he answered.

"And we will not leave too early tomorrow?"

She was worried as she spoke that the Duke might think they had lingered longer than he intended in Venice and therefore they must not stay for too long in Athens.

He shook his head.

"No," he told her, "we will stay here and I will take you ashore tomorrow as soon as breakfast is over."

"*Thank you*! Cousin Arthur. Thank you!"

At breakfast the next morning she jumped up and ran below even though she had not finished her coffee.

"I am going first to the Embassy," announced the Marquis. "I don't suppose there will be any message from Her Majesty, but the Captain is already a bit surprised that we are taking so long on what he was informed was to be a quick voyage to Larissa and back."

The Duke smiled.

"I really think you have made the journey far more pleasant than it might have been."

"It is still unmitigated hell," the Marquis muttered and he walked out of the Saloon before the Duke could say anything more.

'There is nothing I can do,' the Duke mumbled to himself, 'except to hope that Valona's prophecy will come true.'

60

He had been told by Rose and Gerald what Valona had said and he did not believe a word of it.

He had heard so many predictions about horses as to which would quite certainly win the Grand National, or the Gold Cup at Ascot and the poor owner was often very disappointed when the day came.

He had also proved to himself that it was almost impossible to win at roulette – the lucky charms which so many punters carried with them at Monte Carlo were just a lot of rubbish.

It was just a way, he thought, of extracting money from people who were stupid enough to believe what they were told – they just expected miracles when the dice were loaded against them.

And that, at this precise moment, included his sister and Gerald.

The Duke was quite certain they had no chance of ever being happy together, but all the same, for their sakes, he felt that he must pretend to believe Valona's prophesies.

She had certainly lifted the veil of darkness which would have prevailed over them all until the voyage ended.

Valona now came hurrying towards him.

She was wearing a voluminous sun hat over her fair hair and carrying a sunshade.

"I am now ready, Cousin Arthur, please can we go ashore at once?"

The Duke smiled at her eagerness.

"Come along then, Valona" he urged. "If I have to wear out my feet and my brain in amusing you, I suppose it would be hopeless to complain."

"Quite quite hopeless. And if you desert me, I shall go on my own anyway and you know Her Majesty would not approve of that!"

The Duke chuckled.

"I think it is a very good thing that Her Majesty has no idea what we are doing and I really hope she will never find out!"

Valona looked at him questioningly.

"Because the Queen had forgotten about you and your mother, she never asked your age. I am quite certain, if she had known how young you are, she would certainly have found, even at the last moment, some elderly widow or spinster to be Lady-in-Waiting to Rose."

"And Rose would have been furious."

"I know, but you have been so wonderful with her. You have surely made her so much happier than she would have been otherwise."

"She *will* be happy one day," said Valona simply. "And it is no use arguing about it, just because you don't believe me and anyway I don't believe *you!*"

"That is certainly true, but come on, Valona, there is a carriage now waiting for us and we have such a lot of sightseeing to do."

He was right.

They went first to the Parthenon, dedicated to the Virgin Goddess Athena and on to the Erechtheum with its pillars of maidens.

Valona was entranced with everything she saw and everything she was told.

They were late going back to the ship, but the Duke had decided they would have luncheon on board – perhaps they might go to somewhere amusing for dinner.

Because Valona had enjoyed her morning so much she ran up the gangplank, hurried below and went into the Saloon.

Lady Rose was there alone.

When her brother came in, she asked him,

"What has happened to Gerald?"

"I have no idea. I thought he would be with you," replied the Duke.

"He left pretty early – soon after you," answered Rose. "He just said he must go to the Embassy and off he went."

The Duke looked at the clock.

It was nearly a quarter to two.

"Well I suppose he must have been delayed, but I have no intention of waiting for my luncheon, because I am extremely hungry."

"So am I," added Valona.

She went to her cabin, took off her hat, washed her hands and came back.

The Duke and Lady Rose were sitting at the table and the Steward was bringing in their first course.

The food was delicious, but Rose kept getting up and going to one of the portholes to look out to see if there was any sign of Gerald.

"I cannot imagine what can be keeping him," she sighed. "He only had to go to the Embassy."

"If you ask me," suggested the Duke, "the machine or whatever they use to receive their messages has broken down, or he has been told there is a fire on his Racecourse and all his horses have run away!"

Valona laughed, but Lady Rose looked worried,

"There must be something very wrong. I hope his mother is not ill."

"Is she likely to be?" asked the Duke.

"No, but he is very fond of her. In fact she is the only one of his endless relatives he really cares about and she always worries about him when he goes away."

They finished luncheon and they were just drinking their coffee when Lady Rose gave a little cry.

"Here he is!"

The Marquis strode into the Saloon.

Rather strangely, Valona thought, he shut the door behind him.

"What has happened? Why have you been so long? I have been worrying about you," cried Lady Rose.

She jumped up from the table and without thinking that it mattered, she ran towards him.

"I was so afraid that you had had an accident," she muttered in a low voice.

The Marquis put his arm round her.

"I have just been informed," he said quietly, "that my wife is *dead*!"

There was a gasp.

Then the Duke exclaimed,

"Dead, Gerald! But how is that possible?"

"My secretary has sent me a long cable, explaining that Mavis had one of her bad turns last night and seemed to be unconscious. The nurse left her alone when she went to have a meal. Apparently she got out of bed and left the room to go downstairs. She tripped over her nightgown, fell and crashed to the bottom. *It killed her*."

There was silence for a moment and then the Duke mumbled,

"There is nothing we can say, except, as we all will know, it is a merciful release."

The Marquis was looking down at Rose and with a murmur she hid her face in his shoulder.

Valona did not move from the table as she had been right in thinking they would want be together.

It was unexpectedly soon, but there was no account of time where clairvoyance was concerned.

'I was right,' she thought. 'When I tell Mama, she will understand. The others will think I was just guessing.'

There was a silence until the door opened and the Steward who had waited on them at luncheon entered.

"Now you're back on board, my Lord," he said to the Marquis, "I'll bring your luncheon."

"It is all right, thank you. I had something to eat at the Embassy."

"Will you have a drink, my Lord?"

Because there seemed to be no point in refusing, the Marquis sat down at the table.

The Steward poured out some wine and withdrew.

As soon as they were alone, the Duke enquired,

"Do you have to go back home?"

The Marquis shook his head.

"No, I sent a cable saying it was impossible. My secretary and manager, who are in charge, will arrange the funeral."

Lady Rose was sitting beside him and her hand was in his.

There was a light in her eyes which had not been there before.

Valona knew that the wonder of what she had just heard was beginning to sweep over her.

'Now they can remain together,' she reflected, 'and everything will be perfect.'

The Marquis drank a little of his wine, then he said,

"I have been longer coming back than I meant to be because I not only had to send many cables, but I was also making plans for Rose and myself."

He turned to smile at Lady Rose as he spoke.

She made a little sound that was half a sob and half a cry of joy and then hid her face against his shoulder.

"Oh, Gerald," she murmured. "Is it really true?"

"It is really true, my darling, and that is why I had to plan very carefully what we would do next and I want you and Arthur to approve."

"I will approve of *anything*, anything you desire," cried Lady Rose.

The Marquis looked down at her.

For a moment neither of them could speak.

Then after what seemed a long silence, he said,

"I have discovered rather cleverly, without anyone becoming aware of what I was doing, a small local Church where we can be married immediately without using our titles."

"*Married*!" whispered Lady Rose.

"The Priest in charge is a very old man, rather deaf and slightly doddery and who will marry us without asking any questions and will be grateful for a donation towards his Church."

"Are you saying, Gerald, we are to be married?"

"Of course we are going to be married," replied the Marquis. "But no one at home will know about it until we return, and for various reasons that I have not yet worked out, it will not be for at least six months."

"But we *will* be married?" Lady Rose asked as if it was the only thing she had heard.

"You will be my wife and we will never lose each other again – *never*."

The Duke and Valona had been listening to this as if mesmerised.

Now, as if the Duke had suddenly found his voice, he asked,

"And what about the King? What about our Royal mission to Larissa?"

CHAPTER FOUR

There was silence and then the Marquis said,

"There is only one person who can help us and I am prepared to go down on my knees if necessary to beg her to do so."

He was looking at Valona as he spoke.

She stiffened as he continued,

"Please, Valona, only you could take Rose's place and, if I may say so, you are far more Royal than she is."

"I cannot do it. Just how could I?" she murmured almost beneath her breath.

The Marquis moved closer to her and sitting down in the chair next to hers, he took her hand in his.

"Now listen carefully to me, Valona, from what I have gathered from the Ambassador, the King has not long to live, so your marriage, I am sure, will be in name only."

He could feel Valona's fingers trembling in his.

"If you become Queen of Larissa, you will be in a very distinguished position. If you decide to stay on, you will be able to ask your mother to come and join you. I am sure she would be pleased to make friends in Greece once again and to be with you."

Valona was now listening wide-eyed.

"You are intelligent enough to understand that to be

the Queen of Larissa, if only for a short while, will be so completely different to living in a Grace and Favour house in Hampton Court and forgotten until you were useful to Queen Victoria."

"That is indeed true," interposed the Duke. "At the same time you are asking a great deal of Valona, who only came out here to be Lady-in-Waiting to Rose and we were very thankful to her for agreeing to take the position."

He hesitated over the last words.

He had been about to say that they had only asked Valona because they had not wanted to take someone older who was more sophisticated and who would gossip.

The Marquis understood what he meant.

"We are deeply grateful to you," he said to Valona, "for coming and I shall be even more grateful if you will make me the happiest man in the world and let me marry Rose."

As if Lady Rose thought Valona was hesitating, she added quickly,

"Oh, *please*, please, Valona, do help us. You know how much I love Gerald and how unhappy I have been at having to leave him."

Her voice broke on the last words as if the agony was still with her.

Again there was silence until Valona replied,

"*I will do it.* But I am very frightened that I may do something wrong and you will all be angry with me."

"We would never be angry with you, as you have been so kind," said the Marquis. "And I promise you that Rose and I will do anything in the future that you ask of us, because we can be together only if you say 'yes'."

"Then I will try my best," Valona answered him in a small scared voice.

He raised her hand to his lips and kissed it.

"I can only say thank you, Valona, from the bottom of my heart. Now we have to move quickly because Rose and I are leaving on a passenger ship to Alexandria."

Rose looked at him with starry eyes, but she did not speak.

"I have booked the very best cabins available – in the name of Mr. and Mrs. Sharm, and my passport is being altered at this moment."

"How on earth did you manage to do that, Gerald?" the Duke enquired.

"Quite easily as it happens. I have always been told that standing outside Embassies there are men who will sell you a passport if you pay enough for it."

"Did you find one?" the Duke asked in a voice that was almost incredulous.

"I found a man who is ingenious enough to alter the name on my passport and it is not actually so very difficult. Now Mr. Sharm will be travelling with his wife, whilst the Marquis of Dorsham was alone!"

The Duke laughed.

"I do congratulate you, Gerald, you have thought of everything."

"What I am concerned most with at the moment is boarding that ship and disappearing. As I have said, we are going to have a very long honeymoon."

He saw the radiant excitement in Rose's eyes and went on,

"When we do finally return home it will seem quite natural to all my relations and friends that I have remarried and what could be more appropriate than that my new wife should be your sister?"

"I am perfectly prepared to give you my blessing,"

the Duke admitted. "I can only hope that things go off as smoothly as you expect, but you are leaving us in rather a mess and I suppose we should be angry with you."

"We have left you with a most suitable Queen for King Phidias who, as I understand it, is in no position to complain," retorted the Marquis.

The Duke laughed.

"You have an answer for everything. Valona and I will come and witness your wedding and just hope that we shall not get into trouble over it in the future."

"Of course I want you for my Best Man, Arthur."

"And I want dearest Valona to support me," Lady Rose exclaimed.

"Then put on your hats and coats at once as I have a carriage waiting for us on the quay," urged the Marquis.

The two girls rose to their feet.

As they did so the Duke enquired,

"By the way is it legal for you to be married in a Greek Orthodox Church even though you are not a member of that Church?"

The Marquis smiled.

"You have just said that I always have an answer for everything, Arthur, so I even have an answer for that too!"

The Duke did not say anything, but waited for the Marquis's response.

"As I have explained to you, the old Priest will ask no questions. We shall be married by him, we feel sure, in the eyes of God and to make it absolutely legal, we shall be married again at our first port of call in a Protestant Church or perhaps even by the Captain of the battleship."

The Duke laughed.

"You win, Gerald, as you always do!"

71

"Thus Rose will be tied to me first by the Orthodox Priest, for better or for worse, and for ever."

"Which is the most wonderful thing that could ever happen to me," Rose murmured in a rapturous voice.

She looked up at the Marquis as she spoke and she knew by the expression in his eyes how much he wanted to kiss her.

With an effort he called out,

"Hurry! Only when we are on board shall I know that there is no chance of your being spirited away to Larissa."

Lady Rose turned and caught Valona's hand.

"Come and help me," she begged.

They hurried into her cabin.

As the door closed behind them, Rose put her arms round Valona and kissed her cheek.

"How can I thank you? How can I tell you what it means to me to be able to marry Gerald? I have been so desperately unhappy at the thought of leaving him."

"I am so glad for your sake, Rose, that his wife has died."

"I have dreamt that my prayers would be answered, or perhaps it is really your prayers, dearest Valona. You said we would be together sometime."

"I was certain you would be, but I did not think it would happen so soon!"

"And you did not think it would involve you," Lady Rose added. "Oh, I am so grateful, so very very grateful, but I do not know how to put it into words."

"Words do not matter, Rose, but do hurry or Gerald will be angry with you."

"I really don't think he could be angry with anyone today," sighed Lady Rose happily.

She turned towards the cupboard in the cabin where her clothes were hanging,

"Because I do love Gerald so much I want to be married in white."

"What about your wedding dress?" asked Valona.

"Oh, it is far too grand and hasn't been unpacked."

"Then why not that dress?"

She pointed to a large white gown hanging in the cupboard.

"It's one of my best evening dresses."

"Then why should you not wear it on what is the most important occasion of your life," suggested Valona.

Rose's eyes lit up.

"All right, now I think about it this gown has a lace wrap which will make a perfect veil for my head."

"Then what you must do," Valona said quickly, "is to put that on in the carriage. If the Marquis wants to be incognito and no one is to know about your wedding, you cannot be seen leaving the battleship dressed as a bride."

"No, of course not, Valona. How silly of me."

"Put on your white dress, which I can see is not cut too low, and you can wear a small hat just to leave the battleship and get into the carriage. Then I will arrange the veil on your head and we must find something to hold it in place."

Rose thought for a moment.

"There is a pretty wreath in the drawer. It belongs to another dress that is pink and white, but I daresay a few pink roses on my head will not matter."

Valona found the wreath.

It was rather small, but she reckoned that it would hold the veil in place perfectly.

The pink roses were very pale and there were white ones nestling amongst them.

"You will look lovely!" she exclaimed, "and all you need now is a bouquet."

"I expect Gerald has already thought of it."

She was right.

When they hurried down the gangplank with Lady Rose wearing a small blue hat on her head, the seamen on duty appeared to take no particular notice of the two ladies.

The Marquis was intelligent enough to divert their attention by asking the way to the British Embassy.

One of the seamen, who had been to Athens before, described the way.

The Marquis thanked him and hurried on down the gangway to join the rest of the party who by this time were inside the closed carriage.

Rose was holding a small bouquet of lilies in her hand.

"What about our luggage?" she asked the Marquis as they drove off.

"I have arranged with my valet to take it as soon as possible directly to the ship we will be sailing on. He will inform the Captain of the battleship before he leaves that I have received very bad news, which means I have to return to England immediately and I am doing so overland."

"What are you going to tell them about me?" Lady Rose enquired.

"I am leaving that to Arthur," the Marquis replied with a glance at the Duke.

"I thought I would be left with all the dirty work to do, but I shall think of some good explanation!"

"You always had a most fertile mind and I cannot

believe that it will fail you now. The only really important thing is that no one must know that my wife is dead or that Rose and I are married."

"Leave it to me," the Duke conceded flamboyantly, "and I would like to say that all this trouble you are putting me to is now adding up, in my opinion, to a very generous wedding present from me to the happy couple!"

The Marquis chortled.

"You are quite right, Arthur. Equally I shall expect something rather more concrete when we do return home to England, and, of course, we will come and stay with you as soon as we arrive."

"I shall be very offended if you go anywhere else," smiled the Duke.

It did not take them long to reach the little Church, which was in the Northern district of Athens and almost outside the City.

When she stepped out of their carriage, Lady Rose looked a very lovely bride.

Although, according to the Marquis, they were over twenty minutes late, the Priest was waiting for them,

He was kneeling in prayer at the front of the altar.

The Church was very small.

The carved pews and the ancient windows made a picturesque background for the bride, as did the altar with six candles burning on it and seven silver lamps hanging over it.

The moment he heard them enter the Church the Priest rose and stood waiting for them on the altar steps.

When the bride and bridegroom were both standing in front of him, he started the service.

Most of it was in Latin, but Valona understood the parts which were in Greek.

There was no wedding ring for the Marquis to take from his Best Man, but Rose had tried out the Duke's and the Marquis's signet rings in the carriage.

Actually the Duke's fitted her much better than the one worn by the Marquis.

"You shall have it back soon, Arthur," promised the Marquis, "as once we reach Alexandria, I shall find a good jeweller where I can buy Rose her own wedding ring."

Watching the wedding, Valona felt that the service was very beautiful.

The happiness of the bride and bridegroom seemed to vibrate through the whole Church and she could feel it filling the air around her and moving upwards as if towards Heaven.

It was a happiness, she thought, that she had always wished for herself when she married.

But it was something she would now never know.

Then she told herself she was being selfish.

She prayed fervently that Rose would be as happy for the rest of her life as she was at this moment.

When the bridal couple knelt down for the Priest's blessing, Valona felt as if a light from Heaven was shining on them.

It seemed impossible for their marriage ever to fail them.

When the service finished the bride and bridegroom thanked the Priest and the Duke and Valona shook him by the hand.

The Duke passed him the envelope that the Marquis had given him in the carriage – a very substantial donation to his Church for which the old Priest was most grateful.

Then as they walked out there was another carriage waiting beside the one in which they had arrived.

"Rose and I are now going straight to our ship," the Marquis told them. "I am anxious to be aboard before the passengers who are exploring the town return."

He smiled before he added,

"I can only thank both of you, Arthur and Valona, for making this the most perfect day of my whole life which I shall always remember."

"I am not going to wish you every happiness," the Duke replied, "because I think you have it already. Let me know, if you can, where you are and what you are doing. I will be very careful that no one else will have the slightest idea of what has happened to you."

"Thank you, Arthur, I knew I could rely on you."

Lady Rose kissed Valona saying,

"I am so happy! I feel I am flying into the sky and it is impossible to remember what is happening on earth. I am sure you understand."

"Of course I do, Rose, and I know your happiness will increase day by day and year by year. I am even more convinced of this prophecy than of the one that I gave you earlier."

"But what you said then did come true. Even now I cannot believe I am not dreaming."

"I hope you will go on dreaming for ever!"

As they kissed each other, Lady Rose added,

"We will get together somehow as soon as we come back. You have been the most amazing friend I have ever had and I am not going to lose you."

Valona smiled.

She thought it might be difficult for them ever to meet again if she was in Larissa and Rose was in England.

The newly married couple got into the first carriage

and Valona noticed that the pretty hat Lady Rose had worn was waiting for her on the small seat.

"Don't forget to take off your veil," she whispered.

"I will try to, Valona, but for the moment my head is in the clouds and I am finding it difficult to remember anything!"

The two girls kissed and the Marquis kissed Valona goodbye and thanked her again for being so helpful.

They drove off and having waved until they were out of sight the Duke helped Valona into the other carriage.

Now as the horses started off, he commented,

"The sooner we sail on to Larissa the better. I feel somewhat guilty that we have been delaying our arrival by stopping at the different ports on Gerald's insistence."

There was silence for a minute, then Valona asked,

"Can I possibly do one thing that I want to do more than anything else?"

"What is that?"

"Could we possibly divert a little out of our way to Delos?"

She saw by the expression on the Duke's face that he did not understand what she was asking.

She explained quickly,

"Delos is the place where Apollo was born and is the most important and exciting of all the Greek Islands. I have never been there naturally, and it is somewhere I have always longed to visit ever since I first learnt about Apollo when I was a small child."

The Duke smiled.

"After your kindness in agreeing to take my sister's place, I can scarcely refuse any request that you may make. I will arrange with the Captain that you are able to set foot on the island if only for a very short time."

"I would just love to explore the whole island, but I shall be so grateful if I could go ashore for a while. It will be something for me to remember in the future."

There was a distinct pause before she breathed the last words and he sensed that she was feeling fearful and even horror-struck at the prospect of having to marry the King of Larissa.

He placed his hand over hers and turned to face her.

"I feel we have no right to impose this situation on you, but you see how happy you have made my sister and the man who is now her husband. It would have been an unbelievably cruelty if after all these years, Gerald found himself free but unable to marry Rose."

"I do understand," sighed Valona. "But I am afraid of being inadequate for the position you want me to take."

"I assure you that you are so intelligent that no one could do it better than you, Valona. As Gerald has told us, it may not be for too long and all you have to think about is that you are personally saving a small defenceless country from the yoke of Russia."

"Do you really think it is as bad as everyone makes out, Cousin Arthur?"

"I have heard it is even worse. The poor people in the Kingdoms and Principalities the Russians have already occupied are being treated like slaves and have no way of regaining their individual identity."

Valona gave a deep sigh.

"I can appreciate how terrifying it is for them and I only hope you are right and that my bringing the protection of Great Britain to Larissa will not be in vain."

"I am quite convinced that once you are established as Queen under British protection, the Russians will begin to withdraw. The Larissians will then be given the unique opportunity to develop independently and will not become just another Russian dependency."

"I do hope you are right," Valona responded almost as if she was speaking to herself.

Because the Duke did not want her to be depressed, he talked of other matters until they were back at the port.

"I shall tell the Captain to put to sea immediately," he said as they drew near to the battleship.

"What are you going to tell him about Rose and the Marquis?"

"I have been thinking about that problem. I intend to tell him what Gerald has suggested I tell the King and the Court when we arrive at Larissa."

"And what is that?" Valona asked a little nervously.

"He suggested we say that Rose was feeling ill and saw a doctor when we arrived in Athens. He said it was essential that she should immediately go into hospital to be examined. It was therefore impossible for her to sail with us as was intended. As Gerald has been appointed by the Queen to look after her, he was obliged to stay with her."

"That is very clever!" exclaimed Valona.

The Duke went on,

"It was hoped that the results of the examination, which was to take place tomorrow, would not be as serious as they feared, in which case they would follow us."

The Duke paused as if he was thinking.

"For the moment, because of the serious condition of the King, which we heard about at the British Embassy, we thought it wise to go ahead and make the Russians in Larissa aware that the King's bride was only temporarily delayed."

Valona was listening wide-eyed and she queried,

"You are not going to mention me?"

"I intend to inform the Captain confidentially that if my sister is as ill as feared and has to undergo an operation, you have volunteered, having the same Royal blood as her, to take her place.

"Naturally I shall ask him to swear that he will keep this suggestion a close secret in case it proves impossible for Rose to join us as we hoped."

Valona gave another little sigh.

"It all sounds very complicated and I only hope the Captain believes you."

She looked at the Duke a little anxiously before she added,

"You will have to tell a totally different story when we arrive."

"I know, Valona, but there is no necessity for the Captain to know too much at this stage and when you do marry the King he will just think that we have received bad news from Athens."

"It all seems so clever, but I can only hope that no one realises who Mr. and Mrs. Sharm really are. It would be terribly bad luck if they met any friends when they were looking at the Pyramids."

The Duke smiled.

"If they do, I should imagine Gerald with his fertile imagination will invent a marvellous explanation of where you and I are at that moment!"

Valona laughed.

"It all gets more and more convoluted. My mother always said to me, when I was a little girl, 'one lie leads to another lie,' and that is exactly what is happening now!"

"As long as they are all white lies because we are helping other people, I am not particularly perturbed about

81

them. The only thing which matters about a lie is not to be caught out!"

Because of the way he spoke Valona laughed again.

"We will both have to be extremely careful, Cousin Arthur. You have not forgotten you promised that we shall stop at Delos?"

"I have been thinking about it and as I gave you my word, I will not go back on it. But I am going to suggest to the Captain that, if we reach Delos after dark, you will go ashore first thing in the morning and then we must be on our way to Larissa as quickly as possible."

Valona's eyes were shining.

"All I ask is just a few minutes on Delos."

The Duke again sensed she was so strongly looking forward to stepping onto the island of Delos that she had pushed out of her mind the situation waiting for her when they reached Larissa.

While they were having dinner she talked of Athens and the history of Greece – a subject the Duke had always been interested in himself.

He was not really surprised to find that because her father was Greek, that country had always meant more to her than anywhere else.

"I am incredibly grateful for being English and for Great Britain protecting my family when we were driven away from our home," Valona told him. "But I have never been able to think of myself as being entirely English and I may find it difficult once I am Queen of Larissa to behave exactly as they might expect an English lady to do."

The Duke smiled at her.

"I do not think you need worry. They will find you very beautiful and I would not expect the ordinary people of the country will know much about England anyway.

"At this precise moment they are more perturbed by Russia and the Russian way of life which is moving nearer and nearer to them."

"It must be terrifying for all the Larissians. Surely one of the European countries is strong enough to tell them they can go no further."

"No European country wants a war at this moment, and, as you may be well aware, Russia does not want one either. They would have seized Constantinople eight years ago in 1878 if Queen Victoria had not sent six battleships into the Dardanelles which made the Grand Duke Nicholas turn back when he was only six miles from the City."

"It sounds rather smug, but I am most thankful the Russians did not take Constantinople."

"So was everyone else, but it was a near thing."

Valona fell silent and the Duke reckoned that she was worrying about Larissa.

"You are not to worry yourself, Valona, for once you are established as Queen, the Russians will know there is nothing they can do about it and they will withdraw their agents. It has happened before and it will happen again, as long as Queen Victoria can go on supplying enough of her relatives to play the part of Queen."

"I fully understand how important it is," murmured Valona in a small voice. "But I never thought that it would involve me."

"All I can say is that we have been extremely lucky that you were with us and that Gerald's wife has died now instead of a week later, when he would have lost Rose for ever!"

"I felt sure they would be together and I was right."

When it was time for her to go to bed, she thanked God for hearing her prayers and helping them as He had.

At the same time she prayed earnestly for herself.

'I certainly don't want to marry the King of Larissa. Although they think that he is going to die, he might easily hang on for years.'

Then she thought how terrifying it would be if he did die and they expected her to take his place in ruling the country.

She would have no idea of how to even start.

How could she, having been brought up so simply in Hampton Court?

Then she began to believe that she was frightening herself unnecessarily.

The King had a son.

Surely he was old enough to play his part in ruling Larissa once they were freed from the Russians.

The whole story seemed to swirl around and around in Valona's head.

Although she tried, there seemed nothing simple or straight forward about it.

'One thing I am quite determined on,' she thought to herself, 'is that I shall ask Mama to come out and join me as soon as possible. She at the very least will know what I should do and how I should behave.'

She gave a deep sigh.

'Until she arrives I am bound to make hundreds of mistakes and perhaps have all the courtiers in the Palace laughing at me or despising me.'

The more she thought about it the more frightening it became.

Only when she climbed into bed did she remember that she was to be called very early.

She was to visit Delos and that was more exciting than anything else!

She had a feeling within herself that of all the Gods Apollo would help her. He had always been the hero at the back of her mind ever since her childhood.

Her mother had told her all the stories of the Greek Gods and Goddesses and about the contribution the Greek dramatists and philosophers had made to world civilisation.

She had told Valona how the spirit of Apollo could still be sensed at Delphi in the beautiful valley beneath the shimmering cliffs and how he had arrived in the little town of Crisa in a ship guided by a dolphin.

He had sprung ashore and claimed possession of all the land which he could see and no one opposed him.

So often had Valona imagined Apollo standing in the sunshine with his arms outstretched and the olive trees around him.

She had grown up mesmerised by him.

She felt that he was in some way more important to her than any Christian Saint could be.

And it had always been her ambition to visit Delos where Apollo had been born and from there all the Greeks believed that his influence had spread across the world.

As Valona grew older she learnt a great deal more about Apollo from the big library in Hampton Court Palace and from her conversations with Sir Mortimer.

It was he who told her that from Apollo had come all the things that men needed.

He was the first of the Gods that men could strive to resemble.

From him came science, the sense of order and all that is adventurous and daring in man.

Valona had listened to Sir Mortimer wide-eyed.

Every word seemed more significant that anything she had learnt from her tutors and teachers.

"Apollo was the sunlight of the human mind," Sir Mortimer said not once but many times, "and one day he will be acknowledged for all he has given to mankind and to everyone who has learnt so much from him."

Now she was to visit the island dedicated to Apollo and she would feel for herself the wonder and glory of him.

She had been told that the unique enchantment of Delos still existed – it seemed incredible after the passing of so many years.

No one was allowed to be born or to die on what was known as the Virgin Island.

It remained the Virgin still.

Sir Mortimer had said,

"Divine light falls over it."

Before Valona finally fell into a deep sleep she told herself that it was the Divine Light of Apollo, which would help her through the ordeal which awaited her in Larissa.

If that light was with her, she would no longer need to be afraid.

CHAPTER FIVE

Valona heard a knock at her door.

She realised that it was the Duke's valet telling her it was time for her to get up.

She pulled back the curtains over the portholes and saw that the sun had just risen – it was very early indeed.

She knew the Duke was worried about not wasting time and reaching Larissa as soon as possible.

But he was allowing her to visit Delos.

She dressed herself in a few minutes, not taking any notice of her hair which hung loosely over her shoulders.

Then in flat-heeled shoes, she ran out of her cabin and up on deck, where she saw that they were anchored in a small bay.

There was a seaman to help her down a rope ladder into a small boat where two more seamen were waiting to row her to the shore.

It was only a short distance to Delos and apart from bidding her "good morning," they did not speak.

They ran the boat up the beach and helped her out.

She hurried up a narrow path that led to the top of a low cliff.

She had read in one book that the small mysterious island of Delos lay very low in the water, as the author had said, '*with only the small hill of Cynthus to hold it from floating away.*'

It took Valona a few seconds to reach the top of the cliff and then she found herself standing as she had longed to on the island of Delos.

As it was spring she had expected the island to be a mass of flowers. Anemones flooded the meadows which were filled with many gleaming columns and ruins of what had once been temples.

Looking ahead of her Valona was still.

Now she could feel the wind blowing softly around her and the sense of enchantment she had always known she would find in Delos.

A dozen books had told her that a Divine light fell over the island and Apollo's presence could positively be felt.

As she stood there she could see the light flashing against white marble, which lay visibly among the flowers.

Over the whole island the air seemed to be like a dancing quivering flame.

She could not explain it to herself.

Yet it was there just as she had expected it to be.

Although she felt she must be imagining it, she was aware of the light glittering and shining high up in the air.

She could not explain it, but there seemed to be a mysterious quivering, a low beating of silver wings and the whirl of silver wheels.

She walked a little further along the meadow.

As she did so she felt the shimmering presence of Apollo himself.

As though she could see him with her eyes, he was looking unbelievably handsome.

Behind him lay the many white Temples built in his honour.

As Valona moved very slowly over the anemones she found herself remembering what she had read.

How the Goddess Leto had given birth beside the wheel-shaped lake to the fairest of the immortals and his twin sister Artemis and the whole earth had rejoiced.

To celebrate the birth of Apollo, '*the islands of the Cyclades wheeled round in Holy joy.*'

Strange perfumes had wafted over the island and white swans suddenly appeared on the lake.

Apollo had found his rightful home here and ruled the world from Delos – he had conquered it by the power of his beauty.

For a moment Valona could not see ahead of her.

She knew that there was hardly a square inch of the island that did not lie under the shadow of countless broken columns.

No one lived on the island – the only inhabitants were the grey speckled lizards which sheltered underneath the stones.

Yet in the expectant quietness of the scene around her she became acutely conscious of the presence of some unexplained mystery.

She remembered that in 426 BC General Nicias had decreed that Apollo was not being worshipped properly as a God should.

He had led a large delegation from Athens to purify the island and there were feasts, games and sacrifices and the General had presented Apollo with an enormous bronze palm tree.

He had then ordered a huge statue of Apollo to be erected on Delos to the glory and beauty of the God.

Never had so many precious gifts been offered to a God and when he returned to Athens General Nicias hoped that after all he had done he would now bask in the God's favour.

But the Athenian invasion of Sicily of which he was in command ended in disaster in 413 BC. Nicias was captured and savagely put to death.

The bronze palm tree fell over in a wild storm and the broken pieces which fell near the sacred lake lay there for two thousand years.

Then the island was explored by the English in the reign of Charles I and the French came collecting pieces of the statues and other precious souvenirs.

The great statue of Apollo which had fallen to the ground was gradually broken up and pieces were carried away to England and France.

Yet much of the statue, Valona knew, remained in Delos, but it lay too far for her to go and see.

Yet she was aware that it was still there and, as she had read, filled with a tremendous power.

One visitor to the statue had written,

"*It was splendid in its loneliness, its perfect beauty and its terrible power.*"

Valona was a long way from it and yet as she stood looking towards the East, she felt the magic of the young God once thirty feet high.

She was sure she could see him with his parted lips, his uplifted hands and his eyes gazing out to sea.

More than two thousand years had passed by since Apollo's statue had been erected on the island and yet she knew just as if he was telling her, that time had in no way weakened him.

It was then that she began praying to Apollo with all her heart and soul.

She asked him that if one day he would give her the true love which she longed for and which he as the God of Light and Love represented to all who worshipped him.

'Help me, please help me!' she begged. 'The love I seek is the same love you give to the world and it is even more powerful than anything else mankind could possess.'

She was sure that Apollo had heard her.

Then she remembered that the Duke was anxious to be on their way to Larissa.

She turned around and for a moment it seemed as if she was turning her back on Heaven itself as she walked away from the light which emanated from the ruins.

There was no movement to be seen except from the yellow butterflies hovering over the flowers.

Yet she felt as if the God himself had spoken to her and his arms embraced her.

Valona ran down the winding path onto the beach and the seamen were waiting for her.

As soon as she stepped into the boat, they pushed it into the water and rowed her back to the battleship.

She climbed aboard and murmured, "thank you" to the seamen who helped her up on deck.

Then she went below and into her own cabin.

She closed the door and flung herself down on the bed hiding her face in the pillow.

She felt as if she had touched the stars.

After this she would never be the same again.

The battleship was now moving and leaving Delos behind. Its speed quickened and they were hurrying on to Larissa.

Yet Valona knew she held within herself the Light of Apollo.

Several hours later, fully dressed and with her hair neatly arranged, Valona entered the Saloon.

The Duke was sitting on a sofa reading a newspaper that had come aboard at Athens.

"How did you enjoy your visit to that mysterious island?" he asked her.

"It was the most wonderful experience I have ever known, and thank you so very much for allowing me to go ashore."

"I felt that you wanted to be alone, so I did not join you."

Valona thought it was just like him to be so kind and understanding.

She sat down on one of the comfortable chairs in the Saloon and the Duke said,

"The Captain has informed me that if we keep up this speed we shall arrive at the Port of Zante, which as you know is the Capital of Larissa, at around about six o'clock this afternoon."

As he spoke to her Valona remembered again what was awaiting her at Larissa and she now felt as if she had come crashing back to earth with a bang.

She had been living briefly in the mystic world of the Gods and now she was forced to face the difficulties and problems of earth.

"Do you think," she asked in a small rather scared voice, "they will expect me to marry the King at once?"

"If the situation is quite as bad as our Ambassador in Athens told me, I do believe they will want to make you their Queen as soon as possible."

Valona gave a little sigh, but she did not speak.

The Duke was thinking how brave she was.

He was so aware that any young girl would shrink from the horror of being married to a much older man who was in ill-health.

And not even being able to make his acquaintance first or even become friends with him before she was to be his wife.

He was wondering what he could say to console her when the Stewards came in to lay the table for luncheon.

"I am sure the Chef has taken on some fresh food at Athens which we shall enjoy," remarked the Duke.

He walked across to the porthole and looked out at the sea.

The Aegean Sea was brilliant blue and glassy calm with the sun shining overhead.

He thought it was the sort of weather any traveller would be happy to find when exploring a new country and he himself would greatly enjoy it.

But now there was still the ominous darkness of the Russians hanging over what lay ahead for them, but there was no point in talking about it.

He therefore discussed the history of Greece again with Valona and soon they were both enjoying an animated discourse on the merits of the Greek Philosophers.

It always amused the Duke when he found a very pretty woman who used her brains, as he had noted that far too many of the beauties in London were only interested in themselves and their appearance.

On the subject of Greece they both naturally talked about Olympus.

The Duke had visited the mountain to find it rather disappointing.

"There was no feeling of holiness that I somehow expected to find there."

Valona longed to tell him how different Delos was and yet somehow it was impossible to put into words what she felt when she had stood on the island.

She still felt the glory of it within herself.

The Duke was aware that there was a reserve about her that had not been there before, so he deliberately turned the conversation to other matters.

When luncheon was over they went up on deck.

There was little to see except the blue sea through which they were moving at what the Captain said proudly was a record speed.

"We will certainly be at Zante, Your Grace, by six o'clock, if not earlier," he boasted.

"I do congratulate you, Captain, I had no idea that these heavily armoured battleships could travel so fast."

He realised that his praise pleased the Captain and after paying him several more compliments he and Valona went below.

"I am hoping to write a letter to Mama," she said. "I hope if we post it as soon as we arrive, it will not take too long to reach her."

The Duke picked up the newspaper again, while she sat down at the writing desk.

She wrote two pages to her mother, telling her what she had seen in Athens and also a little about Delos.

She did not mention what had happened with Lady Rose and the Marquis, knowing that was a secret – it must not be revealed to anyone till the Duke gave her permission to do so.

This meant that she could not tell her mother either that she had agreed to marry the King in Rose's place.

Then as she signed her name with endless love and kisses she was aware that the battleship was slowing down.

She was about to say that it seemed a little strange, when she looked round and saw that the Duke was asleep.

She therefore started another page of her letter and told her mother how very kind and considerate the Duke had been to her.

The only good news she could think of concerning her own future was that her mother would doubtless enjoy coming out to Larissa.

The engines of the battleship, having slowed down, started up again.

As they did so, the Duke woke up.

"Have I been asleep?" he muttered.

"You have," answered Valona, "and I think it must have been the engines that woke you."

"Engines? What do you mean?"

Before Valona could explain the door of the Saloon opened.

The Steward announced,

"His Royal Highness Prince Ajax, Your Grace."

Both the Duke and Valona stared at the newcomer in astonishment.

Then, as he entered the Saloon, Valona gave a gasp.

For one moment she thought she must be dreaming and imagining what she saw.

The man joining them seemed to be her image of Apollo himself.

The Duke and Valona rose to their feet as Prince Ajax came towards them.

It was then that Valona told herself her eyes must have deceived her – it was a tall, exceedingly handsome young man who had just joined them, but not the God of whom she was still dreaming.

The Duke looked at him in surprise and asked,

"How is it possible that Your Royal Highness has joined us?"

The newcomer smiled.

"I have been watching and waiting for you for what seemed to me to be a very long time."

"I must apologise for that, Your Royal Highness," replied the Duke. "I am afraid that we have taken longer in coming from London than we expected."

"I was reckoning on your arrival almost a week ago and I have had three ships looking out for you and waiting to flag your approach if it was in daylight or to send a ball of fire into the sky if you came at night."

He gave a sigh of relief and continued,

"But now you are here and I can only say how glad and grateful I am to see you!"

As he spoke Prince Ajax looked towards Valona.

Hastily, the Duke, although still astonished by the Prince's arrival, announced,

"May I please be permitted to present Her Royal Highness, Princess Valona?"

Valona curtsied and the Prince bowed.

"May I offer you some refreshment?"

"I have come aboard now," he said, "because it is essential that you should understand the situation we are in before you actually arrive in Larissa."

"Perhaps Your Royal Highness would prefer to sit down," offered the Duke, indicating the sofa.

Prince Ajax did as was suggested and the Duke sat beside him with Valona in an armchair close to them.

There was silence for a moment and then he looked at the door.

"I presume that no one can hear us and it is safe for me to speak."

"Quite safe, Your Royal Highness."

Valona noticed from the expression in the Duke's eyes that he was surprised by the Prince's demeanour.

Again there was a somewhat uncomfortable silence, before Prince Ajax began,

"Perhaps it would be best also for your sister, Lady Rose, and the Marquis of Dorsham, the representative of Her Majesty, to hear what I have to say."

The Duke held his breath.

"If you would excuse the suggestion, Your Royal Highness," he replied, "it would be best if the Princess and I heard what you have to say in case it is upsetting."

"Yes, you are right," agreed Prince Ajax.

Once again he looked towards the door as if he was afraid that someone might be listening.

Then in a low voice, he announced,

"I have come to tell you that my father, the King, is *dead*!"

The Duke started.

"Dead, Your Royal Highness?"

"He died yesterday morning, but, as we have feared for at least a week, there was no chance of saving him.

"You can understand that the situation in Larissa is now more dangerous than ever. The Prime Minister and the Chiefs of Staff are all convinced that the moment the Russians learn of my father's death, they will begin their move to take over the country."

Valona clasped her hands together.

After a pause the Duke enquired,

"I presume that Your Royal Highness is now taking every precaution to prevent them from doing so."

"The only deterrence to really prevent them would have been my father's marriage to Lady Rose. Now, as I am King, it must be *mine*."

For a moment the Duke stared at him.

"Yes, of course, I understand."

"What we are afraid of," he resumed, "is that they will strike before the marriage actually takes place. That is why no one else, with the exception of my father's doctor and his valet, knows that he is dead."

The Duke stared at him.

"Surely it has been very difficult to keep the news a secret."

"It has been difficult because you did not arrive at the time we expected you. But now you are here, I have made arrangements to which I hope you will agree."

"What are they?" enquired the Duke.

"The marriage will take place tomorrow morning and no one in the whole of Larissa will have any idea that my father is not the bridegroom.

"I am fighting for my people's lives and my own and I assure you the only way I can save my country is to make the Russians realise we are now under the protection of Great Britain."

"So Your Royal Highness will be married in your father's place," the Duke stated, as if he was determined to get it completely clear in his own mind.

"That is correct and immediately that the Marriage Service has ended, I and Lady Rose will be crowned King and Queen of Larissa."

The Duke could see it was a very astute plan if the Russians were kept in ignorance of what was happening.

But Prince Ajax had referred to his sister, assuming that she was on board.

"I have something to tell Your Royal Highness, but I do not think it will interfere with your plan."

"What is it?" the Prince asked a little sharply.

It made Valona believe that he was nervous in case his plan, which he had obviously thought out so carefully, could not be carried out.

"My sister was taken seriously ill while we were in Athens and the doctors claimed it was impossible for her to travel any further and essential that she should remain in their care."

"Are you now telling me that your sister is *not* with you?" Prince Ajax demanded.

There was a note of horror in his voice which made the Duke respond quickly,

"My sister regrettably is not with us, but Princess Valona, the daughter of the late Prince and the Princess of Piracus is prepared to take her place. She is in point of fact more closely related to Queen Victoria than my sister."

The Prince now turned round to look at Valona and he gave her a long searching look.

Then he said in a different tone,

"I can only thank you, Your Royal Highness, and I will be exceedingly grateful if you will take Lady Rose's place."

"I will most certainly do so," responded Valona in a low voice, "because I realise it is the only way Your Royal Highness can save your country."

"It is indeed the only way," he repeated. "And as I have already said, we must be married tomorrow morning. No one in the Palace will have the least idea until the very last moment that I am taking my father's place."

"I do understand," muttered Valona.

For the first time Prince Ajax smiled at her.

"I believed you would and I remember how bravely your father fought against all the rebels in his country, but sadly they succeeded in throwing him off his throne."

"And wounding him first," added Valona, "so that he died soon after we arrived in England."

"I am sure your father would not want Larissa to be taken over by the Russians. We therefore have to be very clever and outwit them, although I am afraid it is not going to be easy."

"Surely Your Royal Highness is ready to thwart the Russians?" the Duke asked.

There was a little pause before he answered,

"I am afraid, as my father has been so ill for some time, that we have been most remiss in not enlarging the Army or bringing it up-to-date with modern weapons."

The Duke looked worried and Prince Ajax went on,

"I have been travelling abroad as I wanted to see something of the world, and actually you do not remember me, but I was at Oxford University at the same time as you were."

The Duke looked amazed.

"You were!"

"I was at a not very important College and I was not skilled as you were on the cricket field, nor did I row in the Oxford boat against Cambridge."

The Duke smiled.

He had been Captain of Cricket for one season and a keen rower.

"I am sure I would have remembered Your Royal Highness if we had ever met. But as we both know Oxford is a large collection of men and one is inclined to keep with those in one's own College."

"But his having been at Oxford," remarked Valona, "explains why His Royal Highness speaks such excellent English."

She gave Prince Ajax a little smile as she added,

"I have been struggling at learning your language before I arrived just in case no one could understand what I wanted or what I was trying to say."

"It will give great pleasure to my people if you can speak to them our language," Prince Ajax enthused. "And I must thank you again for coming to our rescue."

He rose to his feet and walked to a porthole.

"We shall be coming into port in five minutes time and I have to tell you who will be waiting to greet you on your arrival."

"That, of course, will be most helpful, Your Royal Highness," replied the Duke. "In fact Valona has prepared a little speech in your language if any of your people will be making one to her."

"The Prime Minister will do that and he will have five or six Members of the Cabinet with him."

He hesitated for a moment and then he added,

"I think it would be a great mistake to explain that the bride has been changed at the last moment. Anything unusual happening, when the Russians learn about it, might prompt them to take immediate action."

The Duke stiffened at the last words.

"So you do expect them to take action?"

"I have tried to take every precaution possible, but what we were really afraid of was that they would attempt to kill my father before he could reach the Cathedral for his marriage. Once he was dead, their attention would then be turned to me and I would undoubtedly die as well. As it is, I think the odds against my surviving are pretty short."

"That is wrong," exclaimed Valona unexpectedly. "I know you would love to be the King of your country and make it great again."

Prince Ajax looked at her in surprise and the Duke explained,

"The Princess herself is half Greek and possesses a unique gift of clairvoyance. If she makes any prediction it invariably comes true – almost uncannily so."

He looked at Valona as he spoke and knew that she was thinking of how she had assured Rose that she would eventually marry the Marquis and it had happened so very quickly that they could hardly believe it.

"What you have said is most reassuring," continued Prince Ajax. "Equally we must take no chances, so would you mind if my people waiting for you think you are the Duke's sister, which is who they are expecting?

"When we are married you can use your own name and we will explain later that Rose was the second name you were baptised with."

"Very well," she agreed, "but it makes everything seem unreal and I can hardly believe it is all happening."

As she was speaking she realised that they would never understand what she had felt at Delos.

It was thus something she could tell no one and yet to her it had been completely and absolutely real.

Just as this strange and complicated plot was true even though it was hard to comprehend.

"As you can imagine," the Prince was saying, "my people do not understand English titles and they have been speaking of Lady Rose as a Princess. I therefore think it is easier, until you later become Queen, that I refer to you as Princess Rose. When the crown is on our heads we can say you prefer to use your other name of Valona."

Valona made a little gesture with her hands.

"I will just leave it all in the hands of Your Royal Highness and I think we must just pray that our wedding goes off without any interruptions."

"I have planned it all down to the smallest detail, including a large number of Union Jacks, which will not only decorate the route to the Cathedral, but will also be in the possession of children who will wave them as you pass by."

Valona realised it would be a great mistake for the people as well as the Russians not to think she was entirely English.

The battleship was now slowing down and Prince Ajax said,

"Now we are moving into the port and are you both ready to come ashore?"

Valona gave a little cry.

"I must put on my hat!"

She hurried into the Captain's cabin to find that her clothes had already been packed by the Duke's valet and taken up on deck.

Her hat was laying waiting for her on the side of the bed and beside it were her handbag and her gloves.

She glanced at herself in the mirror.

As she did so she thought it was a good thing that her mother did not realise how dangerous her position was going to be in Larissa.

Prince Ajax had not said so, but she was well aware that the Russians might try to shoot her so as to prevent the King from marrying her.

They would do it in some cunning way that would make it appear to have been an accident – or she might just disappear.

Whichever way it was, it would prevent the Royal marriage taking place and the patronage of Great Britain.

This was the one outcome that the Larissians were really afraid of.

She felt a little quiver of fear run through her.

'I have to be brave and resolute,' she told herself.

Then almost as if she could see him, she felt that Apollo was smiling at her.

He was assuring her of her safety.

'*You will be Queen of Larissa,*' he was telling her, just as she had told the Prince that he would be the King.

The Duke opened the cabin door.

"Are you ready, Valona?"

Valona picked up her bag and gloves.

"Yes, I am ready."

The Duke took her hand in his, as she realised that Prince Ajax had gone ahead and they were alone.

"Don't forget you are now my sister," he reminded her, "and let me say I am very proud of you."

"I hope you will be able to say that again after the wedding is over."

"At least your bridegroom is going to be a lot more presentable than we could ever have expected. After all, having been educated at Oxford, he is most charming and, of course, a gentleman!"

Valona laughed as he meant her to.

"I thought we should get back to the old school tie and the Marquis will be very sorry he has missed meeting Prince Ajax."

"We might well have turned today into an old boys' reunion!" smiled the Duke as they walked up to the deck.

Prince Ajax had already run down the gangway and was speaking to a number of distinguished-looking men.

Beside them there were children holding bouquets and at a quick glance Valona could see a few Union Jacks waving on the quay.

"Do we go ahead, brother Arthur?" she asked.

"Naturally, sister," smiled the Duke.

They slowly started to walk hand in hand down the gangway.

Valona already knew that the battleship was staying until after the wedding and there was therefore no reason to say goodbye to any of the Officers on board as yet.

A small child with a bouquet of lilies was waiting for her at the bottom of the gangway.

Valona sent up a little prayer for help.

Although it was the way she had always prayed this prayer was definitely directed to Apollo.

She accepted the bouquet and then stepped onto the platform.

Prince Ajax presented the Prime Minister to her and the formality of the ceremony began.

He greeted Valona and the Duke on behalf of his father the King and welcomed them to Larissa as did all his people.

They were more grateful than he could possibly say to Her Majesty Queen Victoria for her blessing the union between the King of Larissa and one of her close relatives.

Next the Larissa Cabinet were presented to Valona, followed by the Lord Chamberlain, the General in charge of the Army and the Admiral of the Fleet, which, she found out later, consisted of only two rather small gunboats.

There were carriages waiting to convey them to the

Palace and although the sun was shining and it was warm, they were all closed carriages.

Valona knew this was because they were afraid that the Russians might assassinate her before the wedding took place.

Prince Ajax was clearly taking no chances.

As his father's representative he sat beside Valona in the first carriage with the Duke opposite them, his back to the horses.

There were not very many people on the roads and he explained that was because they had been expecting the battleship to arrive a few days earlier.

The Duke and Valona were aware that Prince Ajax had worked out exactly how long it would take a battleship to steam from England to Larissa unless it was delayed on the way.

It was impossible for them to explain why they had been delayed – so they merely ignored the expressions of surprise from all the members of the Government that the voyage should have taken so long.

The Prince pointed out various places of interest as they drove to the Palace and Valona could see that the City was a very attractive one.

There were tall trees on both sides of the road and a great many shrubs were in bloom – in fact there seemed to be a profusion of flowers everywhere.

When they turned in at the gates of the Palace, she gave a little cry of delight.

The whole drive up to the front door was a mass of flowers of every colour.

"It is so beautiful," exclaimed Valona.

"I thought you would think so," said Prince Ajax. "My mother was an ardent gardener and I know you will enjoy the big lake at the back of the Palace and the cascade which runs down from the woods."

"I want to see it all and if it is all as lovely as this, it will be difficult to find words to describe it."

"I will show it all to you, but *after* we are married."

The way the Prince spoke told Valona that he was afraid for her to go into the garden.

She guessed without him saying any more that she would stay a prisoner in the Palace until after tomorrow's ceremony.

The Palace itself was very attractive, but was not particularly large and it was built of a white stone which made Valona think of Delos.

When they entered through its front door there were a large number of courtiers to greet them.

Once the formal introductions were over, the Prince suggested that Valona might wish to change for dinner.

"We are giving a large dinner party tonight and my father is only too sorry he cannot be present. He is being kept quiet today, so that he will be strong enough to enjoy the wedding tomorrow."

Valona realised he was speaking loudly enough for the courtiers to hear what he was saying.

"Will you please give His Majesty my best wishes and tell him I am so looking forward to meeting him."

She realised by the expression in the Prince's eyes that he was pleased with her for what she had just said.

"I will certainly convey your message to my father immediately," he smiled.

The Lord Chamberlain as Master of the Household took Valona and the Duke upstairs and they were shown two large and well-furnished bedrooms next to each other.

The Lord Chamberlain explained,

"Tomorrow, Lady Rose, you will be sleeping in the Queen's room which is on the other side of the Palace. But I do hope you will be comfortable here tonight."

"I am sure I shall be and thank you very much."

The Lord Chamberlain paused.

"His Royal Highness has already told me that your Ladyship prefers to be called by your other name which is Valona. As it is your first name, it is the one you will use when you are married."

"Yes, that is what I would prefer. I think I was only called Rose because I was able to pronounce it when I was very small!"

The Lord Chamberlain laughed.

"Most children like to refer to themselves by their pet names that are easy to pronounce. I know my daughter does."

"Then I hope I will meet her as we have at least one thing in common!"

"You can be sure of that, my Lady."

He was just about to depart when he stopped,

"By the way you will have to choose another Lady-in-Waiting as you have not brought one with you."

"It was unfortunate that mine was taken ill when we reached Athens. Of course we could have waited for her to recover, but my brother considered it might be dangerous where you were concerned."

"He was right," agreed the Lord Chamberlain, "and we will now provide you immediately with two Ladies-in-Waiting, who you will meet at dinner tonight."

"I shall look forward to it."

He left her and a lady's maid who had been waiting

in the background came to help Valona take off her hat and gown.

The woman could not speak a word of English and Valona reflected that Lady Rose would indeed have found it difficult to obtain anything she had wanted.

Their luggage had come ahead of them while they were being received at the port.

But Valona did notice that the trunks containing the wedding gown had not yet been unpacked.

She told the lady's maid that it must be done before she went to bed – the maid understood and told Valona that everything would be ready for the morning.

This was somewhat reassuring, but Valona did not want to think about the wedding which was being pushed through so hurriedly.

Or of the Coronation which was to follow it.

She felt a little shiver go through her because it was all so intimidating.

Then as she undressed for her bath, she told herself she would think only of Delos and Apollo.

She was quite sure she had seen him.

'It is so strange,' she reflected, 'that now somehow Prince Ajax seems more like Apollo.'

CHAPTER SIX

Valona awoke feeling apprehensive.

There were so many things that could go wrong and she felt so helpless because there was nothing she could do about it.

When they finished dinner the night before, she had thought that the Ladies-in-Waiting chosen for her seemed rather dreary.

She hoped she would not always have to have them in attendance as she tried to recall what her mother had told her about the Court at her father's Palace.

As the Ladies-in-Waiting did not concern her then, she had paid little attention to them.

When she said goodnight to Prince Ajax, he bowed low over her hand and as he did so, he said in a whisper that only she could hear,

"You have been so splendid. Thank you, I am most grateful."

She smiled at him and then she turned to the Duke.

"Everything will work out all right," he had told her reassuringly.

She felt that he hardly believed it himself and was only being optimistic.

She now climbed out of bed and had her bath.

Two maids brought in the wedding gown that had been made for Lady Rose.

Valona was not in the least worried it would not fit her, because she and Lady Rose were about the same size.

She only felt, and she was right, that her waist was a little smaller.

The gown was magnificent and Valona thought that Lady Rose had been determined to assert herself as the best possible representative of Great Britain.

The gown was completely decorated with diamante and the long train was embroidered in the satin of which it was made and edged with ermine.

The maids fastened it to Valona's waist.

She hoped fervently that not only would the people of Larissa be impressed by her appearance, but so would Prince Ajax.

Lady Rose had very kindly left a diamond tiara for her, which belonged to the Inchcombe family and Valona made a mental note to be sure to hand it back to the Duke before he returned to England.

It was certainly most becoming on her and so was the diamond necklace that matched it.

'I really ought to stand like a statue in the Park so that everyone in Larissa can admire me as a representative of Great Britain,' she mused.

She smiled to herself at the idea as she pulled on her long white kid gloves.

She was trying to think if she now had everything she required, when there was a knock on the door.

A footman informed the maid that His Grace was waiting in the hall.

Valona took a last glance at herself in the mirror.

Then with the maids carrying her train, she walked out of the room and slowly down the stairs.

When she saw the Duke below her, she realised that he too wished to impress the people of Larissa.

His dark blue coat was all covered with decorations that sparkled in the sunshine with the Order of the Garter across his shoulder.

A diamond cross hanging on a red band was at his throat below his collar.

When Valona reached him, he smiled at her.

"I do not need to tell you – you look magnificent."

"I was thinking the same about you!"

"The Larissians will certainly receive their money's worth where we two are concerned!"

They both laughed and Valona knew he was trying to keep her from feeling nervous.

There was a throng of attendants and courtiers to usher them off.

Valona's long train was arranged very carefully in the carriage at her feet.

It was a closed carriage and she reckoned that, as they were yesterday, all the carriages would be closed.

Hers was drawn by four white horses and escorted by Cavalry Officers riding on either side.

They kept their horses very close to the carriage so it was difficult for the waiting crowds to see them – and she knew it was to protect her from being shot at.

As they were driving along, the Duke commented,

"You are behaving admirably and I know that your mother would be very proud of you."

"I have a thousand butterflies fluttering inside me!"

The Duke laughed.

"I know the feeling only too well. At the same time remember you have Queen Victoria standing behind you and everyone in this City is well aware of it by this time."

Valona realised he was referring to the innumerable Union Jacks hanging from the trees and from the windows of the houses, as well as smaller ones clutched in the hands of children.

The crowds became thicker as they drew nearer to the Cathedral and Valona could see when they arrived that it faced a huge Square.

It was a beautiful building and must have been built over three hundred years ago.

The horses came to a standstill.

There was a long row of steps covered in red carpet leading up to the West door with soldiers lining each side of the steps.

She was assisted out of the carriage and found that there were four young boys dressed in white satin suits to carry her train.

She guessed they must be the sons of distinguished members of the Larissian aristocracy.

They bowed to her very respectfully and there were cheers from the crowd, as taking the Duke's arm, Valona started to walk very slowly up the steps.

The soldiers presented arms as they did so.

The cheers grew even louder as the crowds at the back of the Square could see the beauty of her train.

When they reached the West door, there were four Bishops waiting to receive them.

As they did so, there was a salute of guns outside the Cathedral.

The Bishops led the way in and they started to walk up the aisle.

The pews were filled to overflowing and there were

a large number of men standing at the back for whom there was nowhere to sit.

As Valona proceeded at a slow pace up the aisle on the Duke's arm, she tried not to look about her as she knew that she should look down and appear to be shy.

She had received a message from Prince Ajax while she was dressing – he asked her not to wear a veil to cover her face and she thought it was a rather strange request.

Then she remembered that she was to be crowned immediately after the Marriage Service was finished and a traditional veil would have been inappropriate.

Actually the soft Brussels lace veil falling on either side of her cheeks gave her an ethereal look and it also accentuated the beauty of her features and her very large blue eyes.

When they reached the Chancel the choir started to sing an anthem, which Valona learnt later had been sung at Marriage Services in Larissa for over two hundred years.

Then, as they reached the altar steps, she saw that Prince Ajax was waiting for her.

He was looking just as resplendent as the Duke in a military uniform and his white coat with its gold epaulettes covered with diamond stars and medals.

Prince Ajax smiled at Valona, but she considered it incorrect to smile back at him and merely bent her head in acknowledgement.

Then they were standing in front of the Archbishop.

Wearing jewelled vestments he started the Marriage Service.

As Valona had agreed with Prince Ajax he used her own name first and Rose second.

She managed to repeat the oath in Larissian word for word after the Archbishop without making a mistake.

The Duke gave her away and a tall good-looking General was Best Man to Prince Ajax.

When he put the wedding ring on Valona's finger, he felt her hand tremble a little, but outwardly she appeared very composed.

Then they knelt for the Blessing and as they did so it swept over Valona like a huge tidal wave that she was now married to a man she had only just met and of whom she knew absolutely nothing!

For a moment she felt a sense of panic.

Then, just as she had on Delos, she felt the Light of Apollo pulsating through her.

There was no need to be afraid.

After the Blessing the bride and bridegroom rose to their feet.

It was then that the Lord Chamberlain stepped into the front of the Chancel and a fanfare of trumpets sounded.

When the trumpets died away, he began to address the congregation.

"It is with deep regret that I bring you the news that His Majesty King Phidias of Larissa has died. We commit his soul to God and pray he will find peace in Heaven."

There was an audible gasp from the assembly as he spoke.

Then whilst the choir sang a long 'amen', there was a movement amongst all those sitting in the pews.

They whispered to each other in astonishment.

Once again there was a fanfare of trumpets and the Lord Chamberlain in a stentorian voice proclaimed,

"The King is dead. *Long live the King.*"

As he spoke he held up his right hand.

The aristocrats in the front pews understood what they should do.

They rose in a body to their feet and the rest of the congregation hurriedly followed them.

Everybody raised their right hands.

"The King!" they all shouted.

Then they cheered and another 'amen' was sung by the choir.

Next up the Chancel came a procession of the Chief Officers of State bearing the Crown, the Orb, the Sceptre and the Sword of State.

They were followed by three Bishops, who had not appeared before, carrying the Paten, the Chalice and the Bible.

As they were slowly proceeding, the new King was helped into his Robe of State – it was of crimson velvet, decorated with ermine and gold lace.

Valona removed her tiara and a robe ornamented with golden eagles was placed over her shoulders.

Two thrones that she had not noticed at the side of the Chancel were pushed forward in front of the altar.

The King took an oath to maintain the Church and the laws of Larissa.

After that both the King and Valona were anointed with oil and when they were seated on the two thrones they received the rest of the Royal regalia.

Then the King was crowned by the Archbishop.

A long burst of silver trumpets sounded out and the Archbishop presented their King to his people by turning him to the East, West, South and North.

When he had done so, Valona knelt in front of the King and he crowned her Queen of Larissa.

After which, as the trumpets sounded out again, the King and Queen sat on their thrones.

King Ajax now held the Orb in his left hand and the Sceptre in his right and there was a short anthem sung very movingly by the Choir.

Then with another fanfare of trumpets the King and Queen started to process from the Chancel down the aisle to the West door.

As they did so the whole congregation curtsied and bowed to them.

It was all extremely impressive.

Valona was sure it was King Ajax who had insisted on the Service being cut short – the very long drawn-out Coronation which Queen Victoria had to endure when she came to the throne had taken over five hours.

They reached the West door.

Then as the huge crowd in the Square had their first glimpse of their new King and Queen, the cheers rang out.

They were so loud that they seemed even to drown the trumpets, but the long salute of guns which followed was loud enough to shake the walls of the Cathedral itself.

For some minutes the King and Queen stood in the West door listening to the cheers below them and then they began to majestically descend the steps one by one.

They had not moved far when a small boy of about three years old squeezed past the soldiers lining the steps.

He then ran towards Valona holding out a rose, but before he could reach her he tripped and fell down.

Before anyone could move Valona stepped forward and picked him up. He was crying but stopped to look up at her when she held him in her arms.

"You were bringing me a beautiful flower," Valona said to him in his own language. "It is most kind of you, thank you very much."

She hugged the little boy and he pointed up at her crown and stammered,

"Pretty – hat."

"Very pretty," agreed Valona, "and if you come to the Palace tomorrow, I will find a pretty present for you."

Whilst she was holding the boy and talking to him, the King had stopped and the whole crowd were staring at what was happening.

King Ajax looked around.

"Where is the mother or father of this small boy?"

Two soldiers parted to allow a woman through.

She was obviously poor but she had a clean smiling face.

The King held out his hand to her and as she took it she made a rather clumsy curtsy.

"What is your little boy's name?" he asked.

"Norhis – Your Majesty," she managed to say.

The King turned towards Valona and took the little boy from her arms.

He held him up high and called out in a loud voice, which the people below could hear,

"This little boy is Norhis and he signifies in himself everything the Queen and I intend to do for our country. We want for Norhis and all Larissian children like him to be given a better education, more comfortable houses and above all peace. But we need your help and if you help us, I am sure with God's will, we shall be successful."

He held Norhis up a little higher and whispered,

"Wave to them! Wave to the people."

Norhis did as he was told.

Then he was put back safely into his mother's arms.

"Bring him to the Palace tomorrow and the Queen and I will have a present for him and you too."

The woman could only gabble her thanks.

The King took Valona's hand and they proceeded down the steps to their carriage.

By this time the crowd were aware they had seen something unusual and exciting and were cheering wildly.

As the King was helping Valona into the carriage, he stood for a moment waving to his people.

The horses drove off and they continued cheering.

Flowers were thrown through the windows which the King had opened.

"Do you think it is safe to do that?" asked Valona.

He smiled at her.

"He would be a very brave Russian who would dare to hurt us after what you have just achieved. The whole of Larissa will be talking about it tomorrow."

"You mean picking up the little boy?"

"You have just showed me, Valona, how to reach the hearts of my people. I was wondering how it could be done and you have shown me the way so cleverly without words."

Valona was looking surprised and he explained,

"My father was not very popular with the people, because he appeared only on important State occasions and had no personal contact with them. I was wondering how I could make them realise I intend to reign in a very different way. You have shown me exactly what I have to do."

"You mean look after the children?"

"That will reach their hearts quicker than anything else. I am sure you will find that the schools are inefficient, there are not enough doctors and nurses for ill children and the hospital is only available to those who can afford it."

"Why has nothing been done before?"

"Because my father would not let me interfere and that is why I have travelled and why I insisted on going to Oxford. I was not wanted at home and was never allowed to take part in the ruling of the country."

Valona smiled.

"That is just what the Prince of Wales complains about in England. His mother will not even allow him to see the State papers!"

"I can quite understand what he is feeling."

"And I am afraid that you will be angry if what I want done does not coincide with what you want."

"We will wait and see," replied the King. "I have a feeling that we both desire the same things – prosperity for my country, security against the Russians and the love of those over whom we rule."

Valona drew in her breath.

She had never expected King Ajax to speak to her in such a way.

She had expected because he was an older man that he would be very set in his ways.

She did not think he would listen to any suggestion she might make nor to anything she particularly wanted to do.

"I do want to help you, Ajax, I want to very much. But you must be aware that I am so terrified of making a mistake."

"I think it is impossible that you would ever do so," he replied.

She looked at him questioningly.

By now they had arrived back at the Palace and as the horses came to a standstill, the King said,

"You realise that it is now essential for us to give a

banquet at which I have to make a speech. Do not be too critical, because it is something I have never done before."

Valona was surprised.

Equally she and her mother had often discussed the position of the Prince of Wales – the majority of the Social world in England believed that he was very badly treated.

"Are you surprised," she had heard one woman say to her mother, "that His Royal Highness pursues one pretty girl after another? He is not allowed to do anything serious and I am told he is continually complaining to his friends he is not even allowed to attend Her Majesty's audiences with foreign diplomats."

"I think it is very unkind," her mother had replied. "After all His Royal Highness is getting on in years and it must be very frustrating to know he will have to wait until he is an old man before he may rule the Empire."

"They make a fuss of him in France," her mother's friend continued, "which is why he likes going there. But I contend that it is unfair when people refer to him as being of no political consequence."

"I agree with you, but unfortunately there is nothing we can do about it."

"Nothing," her friend agreed. "And he will be kept outside Her Majesty's confidence until she dies."

At the time Valona had felt extremely sorry for the Prince of Wales and she now sympathised with how King Ajax must have felt.

She could understand him being totally determined to change a great many things in Larissa.

But she knew everything still depended on keeping the Russians away.

They could attack now when the Army was weak and the country had no fleet.

The King could be driven out of his Palace, as her father had been and he would become nothing more than an encumbrance on England or some other country.

'We must somehow find a way of ridding ourselves of those ghastly Russians for ever,' Valona decided as they walked into the Palace.

*

The State banquet was held in the ballroom and there were nearly five hundred people present.

A delicious luncheon was provided for the guests and while they ate, soft music was played by a Regimental band, which had been told on no account to drown out the voices of the guests.

There were many tables with the King sitting at the head of one of them, the Queen at another.

Valona had a distinguished elder Statesman placed on either side of her and they paid her compliments, but at the same time she still managed to learn quite a number of facts she needed to know about the country, especially the way it had been ruled in the past.

She thought that the King was likely to have a great deal of support for the innovations he wanted to introduce.

Yet some of the older Cabinet members would fight hard against anything new or different from the way it had been for years.

When King Ajax rose to make his speech there was loud applause.

Listening to him Valona realised how intelligent he was.

He did not frighten his guests with too many new ideas, which to some of them might seem revolutionary.

Instead he thanked and complimented them on the way they had served his father and told them frankly that he realised, because he had been abroad so much, that he himself had a great deal to learn.

"I do need your help," he professed, "and I need it desperately. I know you will understand that we have to work speedily and be prepared to defend ourselves as we have never done in the past."

There was a murmur of agreement from the audience.

"It will be no use saying later," the King went on, "if anything untoward does happen, that we were just taken by surprise. We have to act now and that is why I need your support, your experience and above all your devotion to Larissa to help me."

There was loud applause as he finished his speech and Valona knew that he had captivated the majority of his audience.

'He is clever, very clever,' she said to herself, 'and I must help him in every way I can.'

The banquet took a long time and ended up with the whole company singing the traditional songs of Larissa.

Some were very ancient songs and they brought a suspicion of tears to the more elderly of the guests.

The party finished with the singing of the Larissian equivalent of '*God Save the King*.'

Everyone present cheered and clapped loudly and drank the King's health.

The King and Queen shook hands with their guests when they left very late in the afternoon.

Almost all of them told the King as they bade him goodbye that they would help in any way he required.

When the last guest had gone the Lord Chamberlain said,

"I do congratulate Your Majesty on giving the best party I have ever known. I think it extraordinarily astute of you to have managed to obtain a promise of help from such a large number of the guests, who I would have expected to oppose anything which had not been tried out for at least half a century!"

The King laughed.

"Let us hope, when they think it over more soberly tomorrow, they do not back out."

"No, I think having given their word they will keep it," the Lord Chamberlain responded.

He bowed low as the King and Queen left for their private State rooms.

As she had seen little of the Palace so far, Valona was interested to see as much as she could.

She thought that the furniture was, on the whole, attractive, but the rooms needed only a touch of colour here and there to make them look more impressive.

"Are you being critical, Valona?" the King asked unexpectedly.

"Are you trying to read my thoughts?"

"I find it so much easier to look into your eyes – to know what you are thinking."

"You mean that when I don't want you to read my thoughts, I will either have to walk about in dark spectacles or close my eyes!"

"But I want to read your thoughts, especially when they concern me!"

He spoke so earnestly that Valona felt a little shy and she wondered how she should answer him.

At that very moment the door opened and an *aide-de-camp* entered, bowing to the King.

"Your Majesty asked me to remind you," he said, "that you are having dinner early tonight."

"Oh, yes, of course. I must therefore take the Queen up to change. Please tell the Chef we will be ready in three quarters of an hour."

The *aide-de-camp* withdrew and the King turned to Valona,

"I guessed that you would be tired after such a long day of ceremony and so if we dined early and had a good night's sleep, you would care to ride tomorrow morning."

Valona's eyes lit up.

"That would be a wonderful way to see some of the country."

"I thought that we would ride along the sands and I can show you how important the sea is to us. But we can put it to much better use than we are at the moment."

"I would love to."

"I thought you would, Valona."

They walked upstairs and she found that the maids had already arranged her bath in front of the fireplace.

She had been told that her room had been changed, but she was on the same corridor as she had been before.

The room was larger and grander than the one she had slept in last night.

She wanted to ask if it was the Queen's room and yet she thought that must be in another wing of the Palace where King Phidias had died.

Although it was closed, there was a communicating door between her bedroom and the one next door.

Valona put on one of the pretty gowns her mother had bought for her in Bond Street.

When she was ready she found there was an *aide-de-camp* waiting outside to take her to another State room.

"I do not know whether His Majesty has told you, ma'am," he said, "but the Royal Suite on the other side of the Palace is to be redecorated. Therefore these rooms are, for the moment, the private wing for you and His Majesty to use."

"I am quite content, thank you, and the rooms are very beautiful."

They looked out over the garden and Valona could see a lake at the far end as well as three fountains nearer to the Palace.

They were throwing jets of water high into the air and it was falling like a flood of rainbows into the carved basins below.

"It is so lovely!" Valona exclaimed more to herself than to the *aide-de-camp*.

"Your Majesty will find the garden very beautiful at this time of year," he told her. "And the flowers in this room were brought in especially for you, ma'am, because Your Majesty is English."

Valona looked at him in surprise.

"Why, because I am English?"

"Because, ma'am, the late King did not like flowers in the Palace, but we were all quite sure that being English, Your Majesty would need them."

Valona smiled.

"You are right. As long as I am Queen I would like every room to be filled with flowers. Not just because they look so lovely, but because they will scent the air."

"That is what I thought Your Majesty would want," the *aide-de-camp* grinned with satisfaction.

The way he spoke made Valona feel sure that there had been some degree of controversy over her flowers, and she thought she would make it clear from the beginning that in her eyes no room could ever look graceful unless it contained flowers.

She had no idea that when the King came down to dinner, he thought that she looked like a lovely flower.

She was wearing a white gown, because it seemed appropriate for a bride.

Although he did not say so, the King was comparing her with the bowl of lilies that was on a table by one of the windows.

Valona had hoped that they would dine alone, but there were three *aides-de-camp* and two of the Ladies-in-Waiting she was supposed to have selected last night.

At that time she had felt too shy to pick them out and had merely asked the Lord Chamberlain's opinion.

Because she was so young he had chosen two of the younger Ladies-in-Waiting.

However Valona thought they were either very dull or afraid to speak their mind.

Anyway the King did most of the talking.

He was giving orders to the *aides-de-camps* about the arrangements to be made for the following week.

"What I wish to do," Valona heard him say, "is to present my wife to the people. Therefore I want to call a meeting tomorrow morning in the Square at which I intend to tell them exactly what the Queen and I are planning for the future – also to find out if it is possible to recruit a large number of men into the Army."

The *aides-de-camp* looked startled.

"Does Your Majesty intend to do so immediately?" one asked.

"I would have preferred it yesterday, but I want it tomorrow and I leave you to see to it that every Officer is informed that he has to be on duty in the Square tomorrow at noon."

It was obviously something the *aides-de-camp* were

not expecting and Valona thought that the expressions on their faces were quite funny.

She did not say anything and yet when she looked at the King, she saw his eyes were twinkling.

'He wants to get them wondering what he will do next,' she thought. 'And I am sure it will be very good for them!'

She was quite certain they had all taken everything very lazily when the old King was ill and there was no one to give them orders.

'Now they will all be woken up and whilst some of them will not like it, the younger ones will thrive on it.'

It was still quite early when dinner was finished and the King announced that he and the Queen would retire.

The Ladies-in-Waiting curtsied whilst the *aides-de-camp* bowed.

As they went upstairs, Valona saw in the hall below them, a number of soldiers with an Officer in charge.

"They will be guarding us tonight," explained the King.

Valona gave a little shiver.

"I do hope we shall not need it!"

"You are not to be afraid, Valona. I have arranged for there to be soldiers all round the outside of the Palace with senior Officers and that means there will be no chance of their being lax or careless about it."

It was something that Valona was glad to hear.

As they reached the door of her bedroom, the King opened it for her.

"Undress and get into bed, then I will come and say goodnight to you, because I have something to say to you."

Valona thought it was a strange request.

However, she did not answer, she merely went into her room, where a maid was waiting to help her undress.

She put on her prettiest nightgown and climbed into the large bed with its golden canopy of cupids and angels.

There were soft muslin curtains hanging on either side and her pillows were edged with lace that she guessed had been made by the seamstresses of Larissa.

She wondered what the King had to say to her.

It was their wedding night.

There had been so much to do and so much to think about that she had therefore not really considered the fact that they were now husband and wife.

Valona was very innocent.

Her mother had no idea that there was the slightest possibility of her being married whilst she was engaged as Lady-in-Waiting to Lady Rose.

She had in consequence not discussed the intimacy of marriage with Valona, nor had she explained to her what she might expect from the man who loved her.

Valona had left England in such a rush and it was only now that she wondered if the King would kiss her.

What, she now asked herself, would it be like to be kissed?

Living in Hampton Court she had never met with any young men – only charming elderly gentlemen like Sir Mortimer.

She did not know what a young man might think of her and, it was only after she had observed Lady Rose with the Marquis, that she realised how much they loved each other.

It made her think that some day there might be the same light in her own eyes when she looked at a man she loved and the man would look back at her as the Marquis had gazed at Lady Rose.

She had been able to sense the vibrations of their love surging out towards each other and she felt it must be very wonderful for them now at last to be together.

The Marquis could now kiss Lady Rose and tell her how much she meant to him and she supposed vaguely in the back of her mind that there was something more than that to marriage.

But she did not know what it was.

Where she was concerned, she thought it doubtful as they had known each other for such a short time, that the King would want to kiss her.

She wondered if it would be like the kiss of Apollo.

Would the light from their love fly up into the air?

Would those near them feel the wonder and beauty of their love pulsating around them?

The maid had left two candles alight by her bed.

When the King came in through the communicating door, he seemed very large. He was wearing a long dark robe which touched the floor.

He seemed almost a little frightening as he walked towards Valona.

He reached the bed and stood looking at her.

There was a long silence and then he sighed,

"I suppose you know how exquisitely beautiful you are? Also so clever that I am finding it hard to believe you are true."

"That is a very kind compliment to pay to me," she murmured shyly.

"There are a lot of nice things I want to say to you," Valona, but there is no need for us to be in a hurry."

He sat down on the side of the bed facing her.

"I don't know of anyone, who would have behaved

so bravely and brilliantly as you have done today. It must have been a most extraordinary experience for you when you did not expect it to happen."

"I never dreamt for a moment it could happen to me when I left London," Valona whispered.

"I know, Valona, and although you never expected to be married, you agreed willingly to sacrifice yourself to save my country. Therefore I am determined to make you as happy as it is possible for any woman to be."

Valona's eyes opened a little wider and she looked at him not quite understanding.

"What I am trying to say is that I have no intention of rushing things. I think, unless I am very mistaken, that we could very easily fall in love with each other. But I do think first we have to find out a great deal more about one another than we know now."

She still did not speak and after a moment the King continued,

"I am only playing with words. What I really want, because you are so beautiful and exactly the right person I need in my life just now, is that you should love me."

Still there was silence.

"I know, if I am honest with myself, Valona, that I love you already. From the moment I saw you, I knew you were Aphrodite herself come down from Mount Olympus!"

Valona drew in her breath.

Then she muttered in a voice he could hardly hear,

"We stopped at Delos on our way because I asked the Duke to do so. When I saw you I thought for a moment you were *Apollo*."

The King smiled at her.

"That is what I want to be in your eyes. Therefore my beautiful Goddess, I am not going to kiss you although it is something I just long to do. Tomorrow we will start to find out what is in each other's heart and in that way I hope it will not be very long before we can find love."

Valona looked up at him with shining eyes.

"That is what I prayed to Apollo to give me. *The love which shines in his Light.*"

"That is exactly what we will find together."

He reached forward, took Valona's hand in his and raised it to his lips.

As they touched her skin, she felt a strange quiver surge through her.

It was very different from anything she had known before.

Then as the King released her hand and rose to his feet, she breathed,

"Thank you very much, Ajax, for being so kind and understanding."

"I hope it is something I shall always be," the King replied. "Good night, my beautiful Valona, and I hope you will dream of me."

He turned and walked to the communicating door and as he reached it, he looked back.

"Just in case you feel afraid, I will leave this door slightly open. If you call out, I will come to you at once."

Before Valona could answer he had disappeared.

For a moment the only sensation she could feel was a strange throbbing in her heart.

She did not understand what it was or meant.

Then she sensed that despite what the King had told her – there was danger tonight.

The Russians might attack the Palace in a last effort to save themselves from being forced to leave the country.

Very quietly, so that King Ajax would not hear her, she slipped out of bed and tiptoed to her dressing table.

She had kept the revolver Sir Mortimer had given her in a little velvet bag and packed it in with her jewellery.

It was there now in one of the drawers and actually it was lying beneath the necklace and tiara which belonged to Lady Rose.

She took the revolver out of the bag, loaded it and going back to the bed, she placed it on a small side table.

She planned that tomorrow morning she would hide it before the maid called her.

At least it was there and loaded in case the Russians appeared unexpectedly and then she laughed at herself for being so fearful.

There were the soldiers downstairs and according to the King all round the Palace.

'I will put it away first thing in the morning,' she told herself.

Then she blew out the three candles and lying back against the pillows she turned over in her mind everything that King Ajax had said to her.

He wanted them to love each other and it was what she wanted too.

She was now becoming convinced that the Light of Apollo was indeed hovering over them and it would bring them the love they both desired.

CHAPTER SEVEN

Valona awoke and believed that Apollo was calling for her.

For a moment she thought she was back in the ship and then as she opened her eyes, she remembered that she was in a bedroom in the Palace.

She was *married*!

The bright moonlight was streaming into the room through the sides of the curtains, as she realised that it was still the middle of the night.

She wondered what had woken her.

Then suddenly she heard a movement in the room next door.

It was very faint and yet for some unknown reason it made her afraid.

Almost as if someone was telling her, she became acutely aware that there was danger.

Fear began to streak through her body and then she paused and thought that she must be mistaken.

At the same time she felt that she must find out if anything untoward was happening.

She slipped out of bed.

And as she did so she picked up her revolver from the side table.

It was easy to find her way across the room to the communicating door – it was ajar as the King had left it.

Then as Valona opened it a little, she felt her whole body stiffen in horror.

Inside the King's room she could see the moonlight was streaming in through an open window from which the curtains had been pulled back.

There were two men standing beside the King's bed and he was sitting up between them.

Valona realised in horror that they were winding a rope around him and he was gagged.

Without stopping to think, she realised instinctively what she had to do, so she raised her revolver and shot the man with his back to her in the neck.

As the sound rang out he fell forward onto the bed and then he slipped to the floor.

The other man looked up and tried to reach for his revolver.

Valona shot him in his left arm.

The two men were now no longer holding the rope they had been winding round the King's body.

As he felt it loosen, he threw it away from him and pulled the gag from his mouth.

The man who Valona had shot in the arm was still on the floor and he was now groping for his gun which was in his belt.

King Ajax freed himself from the rope and sprang out of bed.

In a few strides he was at Valona's side and took her revolver from her.

Just as the man on the floor raised his gun, the King shot him through the heart.

As he did so the bedroom door burst open and the Captain of the soldiers downstairs rushed in followed by a number of his men.

Before the Captain could speak, the King shouted,

"Russians are on the roof. Catch them before they escape and leave two men here to guard the window."

The Captain and his men turned without a word and Valona could hear them running down the passage.

As two soldiers remained behind at the window, the King put his arm round Valona's shoulder.

He pulled her gently into her own bedroom closing the door behind them.

"Have they – hurt you?" Valona asked tremulously.

It was difficult for her to speak and her voice was little above a whisper.

"You have saved my life," replied the King. "And it was incredibly brave of you."

"Just how could they have come into your bedroom without anyone seeing them?" gasped Valona.

"They came down from the roof and they intended to remove me that way once I was tied up."

Because it was all so horrifying Valona hid her face against his shoulder.

The King found that her whole body was trembling, so he picked her up in his arms and carried her to her bed.

He set her down gently and she held onto him as if she was afraid to lose him.

"Are you quite sure you are safe, Ajax?" she asked again.

"I am safe, entirely thanks to you, Valona."

Then his lips were on hers.

It was a gentle kiss, but it gave Valona a feeling she had never known before.

It flashed through her mind that it was the Light of Apollo.

Because her lips were soft, tender and innocent, the King's kisses became more possessive.

He too could feel a wonder he had never known in his whole life.

When he raised his head, he asked in a deep voice,

"How can you be so wonderful and different from what anyone would expect from someone so young?"

"Are you really sure you are safe, Ajax? Suppose the Russians on the roof came to find you again."

"I cannot believe our men will let them escape, but if they do, you will just have to protect me again as you did just now!"

He felt a little shiver surge through Valona and he said to her soothingly,

"It is all over. I don't want you to be so frightened and I intend to make sure this will never happen again."

"How can you be sure?"

"We are now going to protect ourselves much more effectively and you will help me to be rid of the Russians for ever."

"I am so frightened," whispered Valona, "very very frightened."

The King kissed her again.

He made it impossible for her to think of anything but the wonder of their kisses.

When he set her free, she would have fallen back against the pillows if she had not held on to him.

As she did so there was a knock on the door and it made her start.

Fear came back in her voice as she enquired,

"Who is it?"

"I think it will be a report of what has happened on the roof."

The King would have moved away from her, but Valona held onto him.

"Don't leave me! Please don't leave me now!" she begged.

"I have no intention of leaving you, Valona. Light the candles and I must find out what has happened."

He walked to the door and before he opened it, he asked,

"Who is it?"

"Captain Ruphia, Your Majesty," came the reply.

The King then opened the door and the Captain was standing outside alone.

"I thought Your Majesty would want to know," he said, "that we have killed all the Russians who were on the roof. I think they must have climbed up from the kitchen side of the Palace, which was not so well guarded."

The King's lips tightened for a moment and then he ordered,

"Inform the men guarding the outside of the Palace what has happened. Next go and wake the Commander-in-Chief. Report the situation and say on my instructions that he is to rouse every Officer and soldier available."

He paused for a moment before continuing,

"He is also to arrange with the Lord Chamberlain and the Prime Minister to issue a decree in my name saying that, because I have been attacked personally by Russians, every Russian is to leave Larissa within the next two days. Anyone who does not do so will be arrested or shot."

The Captain, who had been listening intently, drew in his breath.

"Do we have sufficient soldiers, Your Majesty, to carry out such an order?"

"Tell the Commander-in-Chief that he is to ask for every man who can use a gun to form an Auxiliary Force to assist the Army. I will discuss it with him first thing in the morning."

The Captain drew himself to attention and saluted.

"I will carry out Your Majesty's orders at once."

"Once you have told the Commander-in-Chief what I require, I think it would be helpful, Captain, if you wake the Lord Chamberlain and tell him what has happened here tonight and also the Prime Minister."

"I will do so, Your Majesty," replied the Captain.

"I am very grateful to you, Captain Ruphia, and you will not go unrewarded. You will understand too that my decree about the Russians must be published in the City as soon as it is daylight."

"I will see to it, Your Majesty."

He saluted again and was running towards the stairs before the King closed the door.

When he turned round he could see that Valona had lit the candles by her bed.

He thought as he joined her that no one could look lovelier.

Her fair hair was cascading over her shoulders and the curves of her figure showed through her diaphanous nightgown.

She had listened to the King's orders and when he sat down on the side of the bed, she exclaimed,

"That was very wise and clever of you. At the same time does Larissa have enough soldiers to carry out your wishes?"

"The Russians do not wish to fight us openly. What they intended was to carry me away so that there would be no one in command. I would then either have to abdicate, as Prince Alexander was made to do in Bulgaria or I would have disappeared never to be seen again."

Valona gave a cry of horror and held out her arms towards him.

He held her close and she murmured,

"Suppose they had taken you away as they intended and in the morning we had just found your room empty."

"Would it have upset you so much? After all, you would have been able to return to England and forget about me."

He felt another little quiver sweep through her.

As she hid her face against his shoulder, he asked,

"Tell me, Valona, what you feel about me now."

He waited for her answer, but she was silent.

She merely continued hiding her face.

Very gently the King put his fingers under her chin and turned her face up to his.

He thought that in the candlelight she looked more beautiful than ever, but at the same time he was aware that she was shy.

Her eyelashes fluttered innocently, but she did not look directly at him.

"Tell me," he said softly, "and I want the truth."

"When you kissed me," she replied hesitatingly, "it was much much more wonderful than I ever expected."

"You have never been kissed before?"

Valona shook her head.

"Then I am going to kiss you again, not once but a million times. But I want you to tell me not only about my kisses but about *me*."

He waited.

"Perhaps – " Valona whispered in a voice he could hardly hear, "you will think it is too soon."

The King smiled.

"I think, my dearest darling, what you are saying is that you love me a little."

"I know what I am feeling is – *love*. It is the love I prayed for when I was on Delos, but was afraid I would never find."

"And you think you have found it now?"

"Only if – you love me," she managed to mumble.

"I have loved you ever since the first moment I saw you, Valona. I could never have imagined in my whole life that anyone could be so incredibly exquisite or that I could feel so strongly about you."

"Is that really true?"

"That I love you?" questioned the King. "I never believed in wildest dreams that I would ever find a woman so beautiful, so ethereal and at the same time – so brave."

He pulled her closer to him and then suddenly took his arms away.

"I want to be closer to you, Valona, but I do find it rather uncomfortable sitting on the side of the bed."

"It would be much more comfortable," Valona said in a whisper, "if you were beside me."

"That is exactly what I was thinking."

He walked round to the other side of the bed.

Getting in beside her, he pulled her into his arms.

He felt, as he did so, the thrill which surged through her and he felt the same.

"I love you. God, how I love you!" he exclaimed.

Then he was kissing her.

As he did so he felt her body melt into his.

*

A long time later, he murmured in a low voice,

"My darling, my sweet, my perfect wife, I have not hurt or frightened you?"

"I know now," whispered Valona, "that the Light of Apollo covers us both and we have found the true love that is a part of him."

"All I know," sighed the King, "is that I have never been so happy in my entire life."

"I was very afraid," breathed Valona, "that because I knew so little about love, I might do something wrong."

"Everything you did was sheer perfection and more wonderful than anything I could have ever known."

Valona gave a little sigh of relief.

"I only want to do what you want, Ajax."

"I will teach you about love, my darling, and it will be the most exciting thing I have ever done. However hard we have to work in the day, there will always be a special Heaven waiting for us here in this room."

"Only if we can that be sure the Russians have all gone."

King Ajax was conscious that there was again fear in her voice and because he wanted to reassure her, he said,

"Do you really think that Apollo, having allowed us to find each other and given us so much, would desert us now?"

"No, of course not, Ajax, you are so right. He will guide us and help us so that we will be forever free of the Russians. Then once the country is safe we can make your people as happy as we are."

"That would be impossible, but at least we can try."

He kissed Valona once again.

Then he noticed the candles that had been burning beside the bed had gone out and there was daylight coming through the sides of the curtains.

"It is dawn, my precious Valona, and that means I must be ready to see that my orders are carried out and my plans for an Auxiliary Force have been put into operation."

"It was clever of you to think of it, Ajax, and I am sure if the citizens of Larissa are allowed to fight against the enemy to save themselves and their homes, it will mean even more to them than if just the Army is victorious."

"Exactly my thinking. My darling one, we do think alike and just as our hearts and souls are joined, so are our brains."

Valona gave a little cry.

"That is such a lovely thing to say. Oh, Ajax, you are much much cleverer than I am, but I will try in every way to think as you do."

He could not think of any words to answer her with, so he kissed her again and then he said,

"I am going to get up, but I want you to rest a little longer. I am sure there will be a million things for you to do during the day and I do not want you to be too tired to love me tonight when we can be alone again."

"I will *never* be too tired to love you, Ajax."

As she was speaking, she put her hand up to touch his cheek,

"Are you human, Ajax, or are you Apollo? I just cannot believe that even a God could be more marvellous than you are."

The King gave a little laugh.

"That is just what I want you to go on thinking, my lovely one, and if I am a God, you are certainly a Goddess. Who better could our people ask for to reign over them?"

He kissed her again.

Then as he climbed out of bed, Valona gave a little cry.

"You cannot go into your room unless you are quite certain it is safe and the men we shot might still be there."

Her voice shook as she said the last words and the King replied quickly,

"Forget about them! They will have been removed by now and I cannot imagine anyone else can have entered the room while two soldiers are guarding it."

He crossed the room as he spoke and pulled open the communicating door.

Valona held her breath.

He glanced round.

"The room is empty and the window is closed and barred. I am going to ring for my valet and get dressed."

Valona was silent for a moment, then she asked,

"What time are you having breakfast?"

"I have no idea, but if you will join me I will make it eight-thirty."

"I will join you, Ajax," Valona promised.

As if he could not help himself, King Ajax walked back to the bed and put his arms around her.

"I don't wish to leave you, Valona, I really want to stay here making love with you until it is night-time again. The moment we are free, my darling, we will have a proper honeymoon, and no one will disturb us except the Gods!"

"That will be so wonderful," she sighed.

The King kissed her as if she was very precious and then resolutely, without looking back, he left the room.

She could hear him a little later talking to his valet.

Valona thought it was impossible to feel so happy and still be on earth.

She was now sure that the Divine Light of Apollo was keeping them both safe and he would help them make their country exactly what the King wished it to be.

Valona went down for breakfast a little before half-past eight.

There were equerries bustling around and courtiers hurrying along the passages.

There was a feeling that something important was happening and everyone was alerted to it.

Valona knew it was because the King was asserting himself and dealing with the crisis – he was in the process of creating a totally different atmosphere from his father's time.

The King came in to breakfast and told Valona that everything was progressing even better than he had hoped.

It had been a tremendous shock to the Commander-in-Chief when he learnt that the Russians had very nearly succeeded in kidnapping the King in the night.

If he had been unable to save himself Larissa would at this very moment be under Russian domination.

Later on in the day the King and Queen ate a quick luncheon and His Majesty insisted on their being alone.

Valona learnt from him that his idea of forming an Auxiliary Force was already a great success.

The citizens of Larissa had hated the Russians, but had always been too afraid to say so and now to the oldest man they were rallying to the call to arms.

The King now intended to address his people in the afternoon in the Square by the Cathedral.

"May I come with you?" Valona asked him.

"Do you really want to?"

"Of course I want to be with you, Ajax, and if I do so, the women will appreciate that they are not forgotten."

"You are right, Valona, and I should have thought of it myself. Of course you must come. Hurry my darling, put on your prettiest hat and we will drive there together. I was intending to go on horseback."

Valona gave a little cry.

"I am sure it would be something unusual and make the women feel I was even more effective, if I rode with you!"

The King gave an exclamation of delight.

"Hurry and change," he urged, "and I will give you a horse that is worthy of you."

Valona ran upstairs and it only took her a short time to put on a very pretty riding habit, which her mother had bought for her at the smartest tailor in the West End.

"I have always wanted you, dearest, to have a really well-fitting riding habit, but it has been too expensive for us in the past," her mother had told her.

The habit was somewhat severe, but it had become the fashion. However it perfectly framed Valona's fair hair and exquisite complexion.

The King felt that she looked even more beautiful than she had in her ordinary clothes.

He had chosen a white horse for her that was very highly bred and well trained.

They rode away together from the Palace and onto a road filled with enthusiastic onlookers, who had guessed that something unusual was happening between the Palace and the Cathedral Square.

When they saw Valona, there was a gasp before the cheers rang out.

The King was looking exceedingly smart in his best uniform and feathered hat and he had deliberately put on a number of his decorations, which he knew would impress his people and they would believe that this was a great and important occasion.

When King Ajax and his Queen rode together into the Square, the Generals were waiting for them.

As well as the Army the new Auxiliary Force was lined up on the other side of the Square.

There were men of every age and class, carrying a strange variety of weapons.

They were clearly proud to be there and excited at what was happening.

There was no room for any women in the Square so they were gathered in the roads running into it and when they spied their Queen riding beside the King, they cheered wholeheartedly.

Some held up their babies so that Valona could see them.

The Officers who were not on horseback were all standing on the steps of the Cathedral.

Halfway up there were two chairs for the King and Queen and after they had dismounted, they walked together hand in hand up to the chairs.

Valona sat down while the King stood.

There was a loud fanfare of trumpets and then the King spoke.

There was absolute silence as he told his audience how the Russians had planned to carry him away last night.

"I was saved," he announced, "by the bravery and intelligence of the Queen."

He did not add that she had wounded two men as he thought that would be a mistake.

He told them that her intervention had enabled him to free himself, so that he could strike down the Russians who had intended to carry him away before anyone in the Palace became aware of their presence.

"It is something," he continued, "that must never happen again either to me or to any of my subjects. That is why I have given the order that all Russians are to leave our country immediately."

There was a loud shout of approval.

"Any remaining Russians will be treated as enemies and imprisoned for life or, if they do try to challenge us, I know you will be ready for them."

There were great cheers at this statement and then even more cheers as the King praised the Auxiliary Force.

He thanked them profusely for being ready to save Larissa from an enemy that was within as well as without.

"There is one thing that we can be quite certain of. Now that I have a very beautiful wife from England who is a relative of Her Majesty Queen Victoria, the Russians will not dare to strike us openly."

There were more cheers.

"They have constantly infiltrated Larissa during my father's reign and they might try to stay here under cover during mine. This is what I rely on you to prevent."

His voice was very serious as he added,

"It means that every citizen, man, woman and child in Larissa, must be on their guard and you must be vigilant enough to detect any Russian who attempts to hoodwink us and remain here when we do not want them."

He paused for a moment and then he said in a voice which seemed to echo around the Square,

"Let us clear our country, once and for all, of those who are not Larissian, but dangerous enemies who we have no room for now or in the future!"

There was loud cheering from everyone including the soldiers.

"When we are free of this scourge, I intend with the Queen's help and yours to turn Larissa into one of the most significant countries in the Balkans."

There was complete silence as he said slowly,

"We are a very great people who will go down in history, and our children and our grandchildren will benefit from our inventiveness, our prosperity and above all from the brains and intelligence of our people."

Valona noticed that the men listening to the King appeared to straighten their shoulders.

"We have it in us to introduce whatever is needed in this new world, to dream up many new inventions, new machinery and be first and foremost, as England has been, in bringing peace and prosperity to those who live here."

Again there were loud cheers which echoed round the Square.

"That is the sort of world we want for our children in the future. A world where our brains work not only for ourselves, but for the benefit of mankind as a whole."

He threw out his arms.

"That is what you, the people of Larissa, must aim for and bring up your children to think about. It is only in this way that with God's help we shall enjoy prosperity as a great nation that has contributed notably to the world as a whole."

The cheers were deafening.

Some of the women had by now squeezed into the Square with their children.

They were looking towards Valona, waving their handkerchiefs and their flags whenever she turned in their direction.

"Shall I go down and talk to them?" she asked the King.

He hesitated for a moment and then he smiled.

"Stand on the lower steps and let them talk to you," he suggested. "I am going to talk to the Auxiliary Force."

He walked down the left hand side of the steps as he spoke, while Valona went down the right.

The mothers now realised what she was doing and hurriedly pushed their small children forward to catch her attention.

Soon a large crowd had gathered and the only way Valona could make room for them all was to move back a little further up the steps.

The King returned from shaking hands and meeting the men who had answered his call to arms and found the steps on the other side were covered with small children.

Valona was seated on a step holding a little baby in her arms and there were children all round her listening to a fairy story she was telling them.

She did not see the King to begin with and then she looked up and met his eyes.

She knew he was thinking that one day she would hold his son in her arms.

The colour rose in her cheeks and she looked down.

He thought nothing could be more entrancing.

"I think it is time for us to go home," he suggested quietly. "Is that a boy or girl you are holding?"

"A boy," answered Valona.

The King looked round.

"Who is the mother of the little child the Queen is holding?" he enquired.

A woman stepped out from the others towards him.

"Have you Christened your son yet?" he asked her.

"No, Your – Majesty," she stuttered stumbling over the words as she was so embarrassed at speaking to him.

"Then I suggest," said the King, "you give him my name and I hope he will grow up and join my Army."

"You'll just have to wait a long time for that, Your Majesty," the woman answered.

Those listening laughed.

"What I suggest," the King continued, "is that the next girl baby to be born in Zante is called after the Queen. I feel the two children will be very lucky to us all."

Valona could see how thrilled the women were at his idea and they were stunned at being able to talk to the King and Queen. It was something they had never dreamed of being able to do in the past.

When finally the Royal couple rode away there was no need for the Cavalry Officers to guard them.

If anyone had attempted to attack them, he would have been killed immediately by the crowd.

When they returned to the Palace, the King turned to Valona,

"You were wonderful, my darling. What you have achieved today by talking to the women and children will never be forgotten."

"As I am convinced that the Auxiliary Force will never forget you, Ajax."

"They will certainly want their sons to be soldiers as soon as they are old enough. I am determined that I will never allow a Russian to set foot again in Larissa."

"You are reminding me again about last night and that still scares me," sighed Valona.

"I will see that you are always safe, my precious."

"I am not worrying about myself. If I lost you now I would only want to die."

They were now walking towards the stairs.

King Ajax suddenly turned and opened the door of a nearby sitting room to find that it was empty.

He went in, pulled Valona after him and closed the door.

"Why are we going in here?" she asked him.

"Because I want to kiss you, my darling, and I have wanted to for the whole afternoon and now I cannot wait any longer!"

He put his arms around her and gently took off her hat.

Then he was kissing her demandingly, passionately until they were both breathless.

"I love you, Valona and I want to be with you every second of the day."

"There is always tonight," said Valona very softly.

"And thank Heaven for that. Now I think about it, we should both have a quiet lie down before dinner."

Valona smiled at him.

"I am sure you have a mass of letters to sign, Ajax, and perhaps a number of supplicants to interview."

"They will have to wait – until tomorrow."

He kissed her once again and then he whispered,

"Go upstairs and get into bed, my darling. Nothing and no one will prevent me from joining you in about ten minutes."

Valona gave a little cry.

"I will need longer than that to make myself look beautiful!"

"You are lovely, exquisite and ethereal just as you are and that is why I want to worship you with my soul, my mind and my body."

He opened the door and Valona saw outside there were several equerries and her Ladies-in-Waiting lingering in the corridor wondering what was happening.

Yet they were obviously too nervous to intrude in case the King did not wish any intrusion.

Valona just smiled at them and hurried towards the stairs.

"I am going to rest," she told them, "and I do not wish to be disturbed until I ring."

She saw the surprise in a dozen eyes and carried on up to her bedroom.

Valona knew that the King would be with her in ten minutes – he had said that nothing and no one would stop him. She did not ring for her lady's maid, but undressed and then she lay on the beautiful golden canopied bed.

Sunshine was streaming in through open windows and there was the sound of birds twittering outside.

She thought it was impossible for her to be happier than she was at this very wonderful moment.

She felt certain that she had been right in believing that it was Apollo himself who was showing them the way.

They had found the real love which would be theirs for ever.

In a few moments the communicating door opened and King Ajax came into the room.

Valona felt as if he had brought the Light of Apollo with him.

It was shining all around him and filling the room with the sheer wonder of its brilliance.

As he came towards her, she held out her arms.

"I love you, I love you," she murmured fervently.

She knew it was the only way she could express the wonder and glory in her heart.

The King's arms went around her.

His lips sought hers.

Valona knew that she was giving him her heart, her soul and her body.

The light of love enveloped them both and it would remain with them for eternity and beyond.

As the King made Valona his they were at one with the Gods for always and forever.